THE LAWS OF MANU or MANAVA DHARMA-SASTRA

MAVEN BOOKS

THE LAWS OF MANU or MANAVA DHARMA-SASTRA

John Murdoch, LL.D.

MAVEN BOOKS

Chennai   Trichy   Tirunelveli   New Delhi

MAVEN BOOKS

An Imprint of **MJP Publishers**

ISBN 978-93-90063-13-0   **Maven Books**

All rights reserved   No. 44, Nallathambi Street,
Triplicane, Chennai 600 005

MJP 861   © Publishers, 2022

Publisher : C. Janarthanan

Publisher's Note

The legacy of a country is in its varied cultural heritage, historical literature, developments in the field of economy and science. The top nations in the world are competing in the field of science, economy and literature. This vast legacy has to be conserved and documented so that it can be bestowed to the future generation. The knowledge of this legacy is slowly getting perished in the present generation due to lack of documentation.

Keeping this in mind, the concern with retrospective acquiring of rare books has been accented recently by the burgeoning reprint industry. Maven Books is gratified to retrieve the rare collections with a view to bring back those books that were landmarks in their time.

In this effort, a series of rare books would be republished under the banner, "Maven Books". The books in the reprint series have been carefully selected for their contemporary usefulness as well as their historical importance within the intellectual. We reconstruct the book with slight enhancements made for better presentation, without affecting the contents of the original edition.

Most of the works selected for republishing covers a huge range of subjects, from history to anthropology. We believe this reprint edition will be a service to the numerous researchers and practitioners active in this fascinating field. We allow readers to experience the wonder of peering into a scholarly work of the highest order and seminal significance.

Maven Books

CONTENTS.

Page

Lecture VI.

Lecture VII.

Lecture VIII.

Lecture IX.

Lecture X.

Lecture XI.

Lecture XII.

Review.

THE LAWS OF MANU.

INTRODUCTION.

Sruti and Smriti.—The sacred books of the Hindus are divided into two great classes, called *Sruti* and *Smriti*. *Sruti,* which means 'hearing,' denotes direct revelation; *Smriti,* 'recollection,' includes the sacred books which are admitted to have been composed by human authors.

Classed under *Sruti,* are the Vedas, the Brahmanas, and the Upanishads. *Smriti,* in its widest sense, includes almost the whole of post-vedic literature. The principal divisions are the six Vedangas, the Smárta-Sútras, the Dharma-Sástras or Law Books, the Epic Poems, the eighteen Puránas, and the Upa-Puránas.

Yajur Veda.—The *Rig-Veda* denotes the Veda of hymns of praise. The *Sáma-Veda* contains extracts from the Rig-Veda, arranged for the purpose of being chanted at sacrifices. The *Atharva-Veda* is of later origin than the others. It is sometimes called the *Cursing Veda,* because it contains so many mantras supposed to be able to cause the destruction of enemies.

The *Yajur-Veda* will be noticed rather more at length from its close connection with the Dharma-Sástras. The name comes from *yaj,* 'sacrifice.' It contains the formulas and verses to be muttered by the priests and their assistants who had chiefly to prepare the sacrificial ground, to dress the altar, slay the victims, and pour out the libations.

The first sentences in one of the two divisions were to be uttered by the priest as he cut from a particular tree a switch with which to drive away the calves from the cows whose milk was to furnish the material of the offering.

There are two principal texts of the Yajur-Veda, called respectively the White and the Black, or the Vájasaneyí and Taittiríya Sanhitás. The Vishnu Purána gives the following explanation of their names : Vaisampáyana, a pupil of the great Vyása, was the original teacher of the Black Yajur-Veda. Yájnavalkya, one of his disciples, having displeased him, was called upon by his master to part with the knowledge which he had acquired from him. He forthwith vomited the Yajur-Veda. The other disciples of Vaisampáyana, assuming the form of partridges (tittiri), picked up from the ground its several dirtied texts. From this circumstance it received the name of *Taittiríya Krishna Yajur-Veda.* A more rational explanation is that Vaisampáyana taught it to Yaska, who taught it to Tittiri, who also became a teacher.   Yájnavalkya afterwards, by the performance of severe penances, induced the Sun to impart to him those Yajur texts which his master had not possessed.   The Sun then assumed the form of a horse (Vájin), and communicated to him the desired texts.   Hence the Sanhitá was called Vájasaneyí, and also White (or bright) because it was revealed by the Sun.

Another explanation of the names is that the Vájasaneyins called their collection the White on account of its clear arrangement, while they applied the term Black, for the opposite reason, to the texts of the older school.

The Black and White Yajus differ in their arrangement.   In the former the sacrificial formulas are for the most part immediately followed by their explanation; in the latter they are entirely separated from one another.

A large portion of the materials of the Yajur-Veda is derived from the Rig-Veda, to about the half of which it is equal in both forms united.   But it contains prose passages which are new.

As the manual of the priesthood, it became the chief subject of study, and it has a great number of different Sákhás or Schools. The priests who used it were called *Adhwaryus*, offerers.

Origin of the Sutras.—The *Sútra* period forms the connecting link between the Vedic and the later Sanskrit. *Sútra* means ' string'; and all the works written in this style, on subjects the most various, are nothing but one uninterrupted string of short sentences, twisted together into the most concise forms.   Shortness is the great object of this style of composition, and it is a proverbial saying (taken from the Mahábháshya) amongst the Pandits, that " an author rejoiceth in the economising of half a short vowel as much as in the birth of a son."

Frazer gives the following account of its origin :

" Writing must have been known in those days, but the Brahmans preferred to hold their sacred texts preserved in their own memories, so that as far as possible—for Aryans other than the Brahmans claimed a right to be taught the texts—their power and influence should remain in their own hands.

" Trained as the memories of the Brahmans were—and even yet there are Brahmans able to repeat the Vedic text of their own school by heart, and others who learn the whole Grammar of Pánini, with all the explanations of Kátyáyana, and the interpolations of the *Mahábháshya* of Patanjali—it would have been impossible thus to preserve free from corruption the long prose ramblings of the Bráhmanas and the later sacred literature.   At every centre of Bráhmanism there were schools for imparting instruction in the sacred texts, and from these schools trained Brahmans went forth to act as priests, advisers, and counsellors of kings and chieftains or to become teachers of their particular recension of the *Veda*, and subsidiary treatises founded thereon.   The rules for the Vedic sacrifices, for the domestic rites, for the construction of the altars, and for the duties and customs of the Aryans, were therefore reduced to the most concise and condensed form possible, and strung together in leading aphorisms or *Sútras*, so that they might be easily carried in the memory. These *Sútras* were not held, like the previous literature, to be of Divine revelation. They were professedly compiled by human authors for the convenience of teaching the essential elements of the subjects they expound. So there grew to be different *Sútras* ascribed to different authors, who followed in their teaching one or other of the recensions of the four *Vedas* preserved in their family."*

Besides grammatical and philosophic Sútras, there are *Srauta Sútras*, relating to Vedic sacrifices, *Grihya Sútras*, relating to domestic rites, and *Sámayáchára Sútras*, 'conventional every day practices,' the whole being known as the *Kalpa Sútras*, 'Ceremonial' Sútras.

Monier-Williams says :

"Every Brahmanical family or school had probably its own traditional recension (*Sákhá*) of the Mantra and Bráhmana portion of the Vedas, as well as its own Kalpa, Grihya, and Sámayáchárika Sútras; and even at the present day the domestic rites of particular families of Brahmans are performed in accordance with the *Sútras* of the Veda to which they happen to be adherents.

"Since these Grihya and Sámayáchárika Sútras are older than Manu, they are probably as old as the sixth century B. C.; but possibly the works we possess represent comparatively recent collections of the original texts."†

GRIHYA SUTRAS.

Volumes XXIX and XXX of *The Sacred Books of the East* are devoted to translations, by Professor Oldenberg, of Grihya Sútras, "Rules of Vedic Domestic Ceremonies." They include " Sánkhá-yana, Asvaláyana, Páraskara, Khádira, Gobhila, Hiranyakesin and Apastamba Sútras."

Monier-Williams has an extended notice of Asvaláyana's Grihya Sútras of the Rig-Veda, from which a few extracts are given. He makes the following prefatory remark :

"The Hindu race affords perhaps the only example of a nation who, although apparently quite indifferent to the register of any of the great facts of their political life, or even to the recording of any of the most remarkable events of their history—as, for example, the invasion of the Greeks under Alexander the Great—nevertheless, at a very early period, regulated their domestic rites and customs according to definite prescribed rules which were not only written down, but preserved with religious care, and many of them are still in force."‡

---

* *Literary History of India*, pp. 150, 151.
† *Indian Wisdom*, p. 187.　　‡ *Ibid*, p. 188.

In the *Sútras*, the gods to whom oblations are to be offered are enumerated. They are generally Vedic deities. Directions are given about oblations. The purificatory ceremonies, beginning with marriage, are described. Among them are the following:

1. Ceremony on conception. 2. On the first indication of a living male's conception. 3. Arranging the parting of the mother's hair in the fourth, sixth or eighth month of pregnancy. 4. Feeding an infant with honey and ghee from a golden spoon before cutting the navel. 5. Giving a name on the 10th or 12th day after birth, &c.

The eight forms of marriage are mentioned; the. mode of investiture with the sacred thread; directions about houses; daily devotional acts; ceremonies when studentship is completed, &c. The Fourth Book treats of funeral rites and the four kinds of shráddhas, offerings to deceased persons and Pitris or ancestors generally.

Monier-Williams remarks that the rules of the Asvaláyana Grihya Sútras relating to funeral ceremonies possess great interest in their connexion with the 18th hymn of the 10th Mandala of the Rig-Veda:

" Although the Sútras direct that the texts of this hymn are to be used, yet the rite must have undergone considerable modifications since the period when the hymn was composed."

" We notice even at that early epoch an evident belief in the soul's eternal existence, and the permanence of its personality hereafter, which notably contrasts with the later ideas of transmigration, absorption into the divine essence, and pantheistic identification with the supreme Soul of the universe.

" We learn also from this same hymn that the body in ancient times was not burnt but buried; nor can we discover the slightest allusion to the later practice of Sati or cremation of the widow with her husband.

" The corpse of the deceased person was deposited close to a grave dug ready for its reception, and by its side his widow, if he happened to be a married man, seated herself, while his children, relatives, and friends ranged themselves in a circle round her. The priest stood near at an altar, on which the sacred fire was kindled, and having invoked Death, called upon him to withdraw from the path of the living, and not to molest the young and healthy survivors, who were assembled to perform pious rites for the dead, without giving up the expectation of a long life themselves. He then placed a stone between the dead body and the living relations, to mark off the boundary-line of Death's domain, and offered up a prayer that none of those present might be removed to another world before attaining to old age, and that none of the younger might be taken before the elder. Then the widow's married female friends walked up to the altar and offered oblations in the fire; after which the widow herself withdrew from the inner circle assigned to the dead, and joined the survivors outside the boundary-line, while the officiating priest took the bow out of the hand of the deceased, in order to show that the manly strength which he possessed during life, did not perish with, him, but remained with his family. The body was then tenderly laid in the grave with repetition of the words of the hymn :

> " Open thy arms, O earth, receive the dead
> With gentle pressure and with loving welcome,
> Enshroud him tenderly, e'en as a mother
> Folds her soft vestment round the child she loves.
> Soul of the dead ! depart ; take thou the path
> The ancient path—by which our ancestors have
> Gone before thee."

" The ceremony was concluded by the careful closing of the tomb with a stone slab. Finally a mound of earth was raised to mark and consecrate the spot."*

THE LAWS OF MANU.

Importance.—Burnell says :

" No Indian book has been better known for the last hundred years nearly than the so-called 'Laws of Manu,' and to many people it is still the decisive authority respecting India. Numerous and important as have been the discoveries in Sanskrit literature during this century, and through which a new world has been re-discovered by European scholars, these laws still held their old place in the popular estimation. This is partly owing to the circumstances under which Sir William Jones brought out his translation, and it is partly owing to the high estimate which, in comparatively modern times, has attached to the book in India for perhaps nearly fourteen hundred years. But the grounds assigned for this, as usual in India, are not satisfactory. Sir W. Jones' translation was the first real translation of a Sanskrit work, and for this reason deservedly attracted notice. It threw a flood of real light on Indian notions which had been hitherto imperfectly represented in Europe, and for which the metaphysical philosophers of those days were most curious.

" In India a high position has been claimed for the book for at least several hundred years. This opinion is very fully set forth by the later commentators, who lived within the last four centuries ; it is chiefly based on references to Manu in the Vedas, Mahábhárata, Brihaspati, Smriti, etc. such as : ' Whatever Manu said is curative ;' ' Manu divided his property among his sons ;' ' A Smriti opposed to Manu is not approved.'"

" But the myth connecting the law-book with the Manu referred to in the Vedas is recent, as the real nature of the book will show. That the text owed its popularity in India chiefly to its completeness, orderly arrangement, and intelligibility cannot be doubted."†

Monier-Williams thus shows the importance of the work :

" This well-known collection of laws and precepts is perhaps the oldest and most sacred Sanskrit work after the Veda and its Sútras.

---

* *Indian Wisdom.* pp. 200—202.

† ntroduction to Translation, pp. xv-xvii. Abridged.

B

Although standing in a manner at the head of Post-vedic literature, it is connected with the Veda through these Sútras as the philosophical Darsanas are through the Upanishads. Even if not the oldest of post-vedic writings, it is certainly the most interesting, both as presenting a picture of the institutions, usages, manners and intellectual condition of an important part of the Hindu race at a remote period, and as revealing the exaggerated nature of the rules by which the Brahmans sought to secure their own ascendency, and to perpetuate an organised caste system in subordination to themselves. At the same time it is in other respects perhaps one of the most remarkable books that the literature of the whole world can offer, and some of its moral precepts are worthy of Christianity itself."*

Mr. J. S. Siromani, of the College of Pandits, Nadiya, says :—

" The Code of Manu is not only the most important of all the legal codes, but it is regarded as almost equal in holiness to the Vedas. Every Brahman is enjoined to read it, at least once in his lifetime. A Brahman family in which Manu has not been read for seven generations ceases to be Brahmans."†

Fabulous Account of Origin.—Bühler says :

" The whole first chapter is devoted to the purpose of showing the mighty scope of the book, and of setting forth its divine origin as well as the manner in which it was revealed to mankind. Its opening verse narrates how the great sages approached Manu, the descendant of self-existent Brahman, and asked him to explain the sacred law. Manu agrees to their request, and gives to them an account of the Creation as well as of his own origin from Brahman. After mentioning that he learnt ' these Institutes of the Sacred Law' from the Creator who himself produced them, and that he taught them to the ten sages whom he created in the beginning, he transfers the work of expounding them to Bhrigu, one of his mind-born sons. The latter begins his task by completing, as the commentators call it, Manu's account of the creation. First he gives the theory of the seven Manvantaras, the Yugas, and other divisions of time, as well as an incidental description of the order of the Creation. Next he briefly describes the duties of the four principal castes, passes then to an encomium of the Bráhmanas and of the Institutes of Manu, and winds up with an enumeration of the contents of all the twelve chapters of the work, which he promises to expound ' exactly as it was revealed to him.' "‡

Hindu writers often attributed their compositions to mythical personages, to give an air of antiquity, and divine authority to their works. In Lecture XI. 243, it is claimed that Prajápati " created these Institutes by his austerities alone."

Real Origin of the Work.—Burnell says : " It is quite certain that the text is called Mánava, not from a mythical Manu, as

<hr>

* *Indian Wisdom*, pp. 203, 204.
† *Commentary on Hindu Law*, p. 15.
‡ Introduction to Translation, p xii.

stated in the first chapter, but that it is so called from the Mánavas, a Brahman *Gotra,* and division of the followers of the Black Yajur Veda."* Búhler says that " The Mánava Dharma-sástra may be considered as a recast and versification of the Dharma-Sútra of the Mánava Sútrakarana, a sub-division of the Maitráyaníya school, which adheres to a redaction of the Black Yajur-Veda."†

Monier-Williams says that originally

" It merely represented certain rules and precepts (perhaps by different authors) current among a particular tribe, or rather school of Bráhmans, called Mánavas, who probably lived in the North-western region between the rivers Sarasvatí and Drishadvatí, not far from Delhi and the scene of the great social conflict described in the Mahábhárata. This tribe seems to have belonged to the Taittiríyakas, ' adherents of the Black Yajur Veda;' and their Mantras, Bráhmana, and Srauta Sútras are still extant, but their Gribya and Sâmayâchârika Sútras appear to have perished. In all probability, too, many of the rules, as we have them presented to us, were simply theoretical,—inserted to complete an ideal of what ought to constitute a perfect system of religious, criminal, moral, political, and social duties. Who the real compiler and promulgator of the Institute was, is not known. He was probably a learned Bráhman of the Mánava school."‡

Date.—As in many other cases, authorities are not agreed on this point. It is allowed by all that a number of verses of an early date are included, but when the work assumed its present form is doubtful. Monier-Williams thinks that it cannot " reasonably be placed later than the fifth century B.C. The gods mentioned are chiefly Vedic, and the fourfold caste system is that of the Purusha-súkta. There is no direct allusion to Buddhism, though many of Manu's precepts are decidedly Buddhistic, having frequent parallels in the Dhamma-pada, which indicate that Buddhistic ideas were gaining ground in the locality represented by the Code."§

Búhler says : " This estimate of the age of the Bhrigu Samhitá, according to which it certainly existed in the second century A.D., and seems to have been composed between that date and the second century B.C., agrees very closely with the views of Professor Cowell and Mr. Talboys Wheeler."||

Burnell thinks it a " safe conclusion" that the text, as it is, was compiled between about 1 A.D. and 500 A.D.¶

Later additions.—Under these are specially included the first and last chapters. Búhler says :

" The whole of the first chapter must be considered as a later addition. No Dharma Sútra begins with a description of its own origin, much less with an account of the creation. The former, which would be

---

* Introduction to Translation, p. xxv.   † Introduction to Translation, p. xix.

‡ *Indian Wisdom,* p. 205.   § *Indian Wisdom,* p. 207.

|| Introduction to Translation, p. cxvii.   ¶ Introduction to Translation, p. xxiv.

absurd in a Dharma-sútra, has been added in order to give authority to a remodelled version. The latter has been dragged in, because the myths connected with Manu presented a good opportunity ' to show the greatness of the scope of the work,' as Medhátithi says."[*]

Bühler views the 12th chapter in the same light:

" The twelfth chapter is certainly almost entirely due to the author of the metrical version. Its contents are partly foreign to the Dharma-sútras and partly repetitions. The classification of actions and existences as sáttvika, rajasa, and támasa, i.e., as modified by the three qualities of Goodness, Activity and Darkness, finds no place in the older law books. It is based on the doctrines which are taught in the Sánkhya, Yoga, and Vedánta systems."[†]

Redactions.—Mr. J. S. Siromani says:

" There is a tradition that Manu has undergone three successive redactions. The introduction to Nárada states that the work of Manu originally consisted of 1000 chapters and 100,000 slokas. Nárada abridged it to 12,000 slokas, and Sumati again reduced it to 4,000. The treatise which we possess must be a third abridgment, as it only extends to 2,685.[‡]

Contents.—The Code is divided into twelve Books. Their chief topics are as follows :—

I.   The Source of this work and an account of the origin of the Universe; with a summary of the contents of the whole Book.

II.   Sources of this System and the Countries where it obtains; on the first condition of Life of a Brahman, or that of a Student.

III.   On Marriage and on the Religious Duties of a Householder, or the Second Stage of Life.

IV.   A Householder's Duty as regards Subsistence and Private Morals.

V.   On lawful and forbidden Food, Impurity, Purification, and the Duties of Women.

VI.   On the Third and Fourth Stages of Life, or the Hermit in the Forest and the Ascetic.

VII.   On the Duties of Kings and the Second Caste.

VIII.   Civil and Criminal Laws.

IX.   Duties of Husband and Wife, Laws of Inheritance, Duties of a King.

X.   The Mixed Castes and Classes : Procedure in time of Need.

XI.   Penance, Expiation, etc.

XII.   Transmigration, Supreme Bliss, and Doubtful Points of Law.

Object of Work.—Búhler considers that it was intended to be a text-book for the students of law. " It treats all legal topics

---

[*] Introduction, p. lxvi.   [†] Introduction, p. lxxiii.
[‡] *Commentary on Hindu Law,* p. 16.

more fully and systematically than the Dharma-Sútras. The marks of its being a school-book, intended for the instruction of all Aryans, are unmistakable. We are told, Manu I. 103, that ' a learned Brahman must carefully study these (Institutes) and must duly instruct his pupils in them,' but that ' nobody else (shall do it).' Brahmans are to teach the Sástra and all Aryans may learn it."*

Freedom from Sectarianism.—Bühler says :—

' The freedom of the Manu-Smriti from all sectarian influence is perfect. It nowhere teaches the performance of other rites than those prescribed in the Vedic writings, and it nowhere inculcate the exclusive worship of one of the deities of the Pauranik sects as we find it recommended, for instance, in the Vishnu-Smriti."†

Parallel Passages in the Mahabharata.—Bühler gives several pages of quotations, showing more or less agreement.‡ Instead of the one work copying from the other, he thinks that the authors of both utilised the same materials.§

Language.—Burnell says :

" The first striking fact is that it is in *sloka* verse, and in very simple and modern language. The style of the verses is not at all that of real old *slokas*, but is that of the epics, and a good deal is sacrificed for the sake of metre. Again, the most modern forms of compound words are freely used. The text thus closely resembles the versified forms of ritual Sútras, the composition of which appears to have chiefly occurred in the early centuries A. D.‖

Burnell adds:

" The MSS. of the texts now existing are written in a multitude of different characters, but when the book was composed those did not exist, and it was beyond doubt written in a variety of the ' Cave character.' "¶

Commentaries.—There are several Sanskrit Commentaries. The oldest extent is the voluminous Manubhâshya of Bhatta Medhâtithi. As its title bhâshya indicates, it is not a gloss which paraphrases every word of the text. Its aim is to show the general sense of Manu's dicta, and to elucidate all really difficult passages. It is supposed to date from about the 8th century A.D. Next, but probably at a considerable interval, follows the Manutikâ of Govindarâja. The exact date of the latter is likewise not ascertainable. Kullûkabhatta a Bengali by birth, was the author of the well-known Manvartha-muktávali. He probably lived in the fifteenth century.**

---

* Introduction, pp. liv, lv. Abridged.   † Introduction, p. lv.
‡ Introduction, pp. lxxxiii—xc.   § *Ibid*, p. xc.
‖ Introduction, pp. xx, xxi.   ¶ I*bid*, pp. xxviii, xxix.
** Abridged from Bühler. Introduction, pp. cxviii—cxxxi.

English Translations.—As already mentioned, the earliest was by Sir William Jones, published in 1794. In the Introduction to his translation, Bühler says: "It will be evident to every body how much I am indebted to Sir William Jones' great work, which, in spite of the progress made by Sanskrit philosophy during the last hundred years, still possesses a very high value." Bühler's translation and that by Drs. Burnell and Hopkins were made independently. Both have Introductions, copious valuable Notes, and Indexes. The translation appended is based on that of Jones, edited by Houghton; but the other translations have been consulted and used.

The Laws of Manu, by G. Bühler, Sacred Books of the East. Vol. XXV. Clarendon Press, 1886. Price 21*s.*

The Ordinances of Manu. Trübner's Oriental Series, 1884, Price 12*s.*

The Compiler has freely availed himself of the valuable work, *Indian Wisdom*, by Sir Monier-Williams, published by Luzac & Co. (price 21*s.*) As it is expensive, the reader is referred to an admirable little volume by the same author, entitled *Hinduism*, published by the S. P. C. K. price 2*s.* 6*d.*

OTHER DHARMA-SASTRAS OR LAW BOOKS.

Number.—Monier-Williams says :

"At least forty-seven independent Law books are enumerated. The names of the authors of some of them are the same as those of some of the Grihya-Sútras, *e.g.*, Apastamba, Páraskara and Baudháyana. The same men may have been authors of both Sútras and Dharma-Sástras- Of the forty-seven at least twenty are still extant and are mentioned by Yájnavalkya. (I. 3-5), as follows :—

1. That of Manu. 2. Yájnavalkya (second in importance to Manu). 3. Atri. 4. Vishnu. 5 Hárítá. 6. Usanas. 7. Angiras. 8. Yama. 9. Apastamba. 10. Samvarta. 11. Kátyáyana. 12. Vrihaspatí. 13. Parásara. 14. Vyása 15. Sankha. 16. Likhita. 17. Daksha. 18. Gotama or Gautama. 19. Sátátapa. 20. Vasishtha There is also a law-book, the joint production of Sankha and Likhita; and others ascribed to Nárada, Bhrigu, &c., and Kullúka, the commentator on Manu, mentions the names of Baudháyana, Medhátithi, Govindarája, &c."*

Code of Yajnavalkya.—Monier-Williams says :

"The most important Law-book next to Manu, is the Dharma-Sástras of Yájnavalkya, which, with its most celebrated commentary, the Mitákshará by Vijnánes'vara, is at present the principal authority of the school of Benares and Middle India. It seems originally to have emanated from a school of the White Yajur-Veda in Mithilá or North Behar, just as we have seen that the Code of the Mánavas did from a school of the Black Yajur-Veda in the neighbourhood of Delhi."

---

* *Indian Wisdom*, p. 203.

" Yájnavalkya's work is much more concise than that of Manu, being all compressed in three books instead of twelve. The first book, consisting of 376 couplets, is chiefly on social and caste duties ; the second, consisting of 307 verses (which have been transferred almost word for word to the Agni Purána), is mainly on administrative judicature and civil and criminal law ; the third, consisting of 335 verses, is principally on devotion, purification, expiation, penance, &c.

" As to the date of Yájnavalkya's Law-book, it has been conjecturally placed in the middle of the first century of our era. The period of its first compilation cannot, of course, be fixed with certainty, but internal evidence clearly indicates that the present redaction is much more recent than Manu's Law-book."*

Codes Posterior to Manu and Yájnavalkya.

Monier-Williams says :

" They are all extant in some form or other as described by Colebrooke. Little or nothing is known about the authorship of any one of them. They have arisen from the necessity of finding new laws or modifying old ones to suit particular localities and periods. In order to invest them with antiquity and authority, they are all eighteen ascribed, like the Codes of Manu and Yájnavalkya, to various mythical inspired sages. The fact is, that although Manu and Yájnavalkya still form the basis of Hindu jurisprudence, many of their laws are regarded by more recent Hindu legislators as only intended for the first three ages of the world, and therefore as having no force, or superseded by others, in the present fourth and more degenerate Kali-yuga. Thus the author of the work ascribed to Nárada says :—

" Marriage with the widow of a deceased brother, the slaughter of cattle in entertaining guests, flesh-meat at funeral obsequies, and the entrance into the third order (or that of a Vánaprastha ' hermit ') are forbidden in the fourth age."

" The following acts, allowed under certain circumstances by ancient law, are also forbidden in the fourth age :—

" Drinking any spirituous liquor, even at a religious ceremony; the gift of a young married woman to another bridegroom if her husband should die while she is still a virgin ; the marriage of twice-born men with women not of the same class ; any intercourse with a twice-born man who has passed the sea in a ship; the slaughter of a bull at a sacrifice, &c.

" And the author of Parásara's Code affirms :—

" The laws of various ages are different. Manu's Law-book belongs to the Krita Age, Gautama's to the Tretá, that of Sankha and Likhita to the Dvápara, and Parásara's Code to the Kali age."

" Many modern lawyers, however, regard the whole of Smriti, beginning with Manu, as one, and assert that the inconsistencies and contradictions it contains are all capable of explanation.

" I here annex a few particulars relating to the eighteen principal Codes posterior to Manu and Yájnavalkya :—

1. That attributed to *Atri*, one of Manu's ten Prajápatis (I. 35), is in verse, and written in a perspicuous style. 2. That of *Vishnu* is also in verse,

---

* *Indian Wisdom*, pp. 291, 292. Abridged.

and is regarded as an excellent treatise, an abridgment of which is also extant. 3. That of Hárítá, on the contrary is in prose, but has been abridged in a metrical form. 4. That of *Usanas* or Sukra is in verse, and an abridgment is extant. 5. A short treatise of about seventy verses is ascribed to *Angiras*, one of Manu's Prajápatis and Maharshis (I. 35). 6. A tract, consisting of one hundred verses, commented on by Kullúka-bhatta, is mythically attributed to *Yama* (brother of Manu Vaivasvata) ruler of the world of spirits. 7. That of Apastamba is in prose, but an abridgment in verse also exists. 8. Samvarta's Code has also a metrical abridgment. 9. *Kátyáyana's* law-treatise is full and perspicuous. 10. *Vrihaspati's* has been abridged, and it is doubtful whether we possess the abridgment or the Code itself. 11. *Parásara's* treatise is regarded by some as the highest authority for the Kali or fourth age of the world. It has been commented on by Mádhavácbárya. 12. A law-treatise is ascribed to the celebrated Vyása, son of Parásara. 13, 14. Two separate tracts in verse by *Sankha* and *Likhita* exist, but their joint treatise in prose is the one usually cited by Kullúka and others. It is supposed to be adapted to the Dvápara age. 15. A code in verse, of no special interest, is attributed to *Daksha*, one of Manu's Prajápatis. 16. A prose treatise written in a clear style bears the name of *Gautama*. It is held to have been written for the Tretá age. 17. *Sátátapa's* Code is chiefly on penance and expiation. There is an abridgment of it in verse. 18. The treatise attributed to Vasishtha, another of Manu's Prajápatis, is a mixture of prose and verse.

" Of other Codes ascribed to various mythical lawgivers in the Padma Puráua, &c., it will be sufficient to mention those of Maríchi, Pulastya, Bhrigu, Nárada, Kasyapa, Visvámitra, Gárgya, Baudháyana, Paithínasi, Sumantu, Lokákshi, Kuthumi, and Dhaumya."

" Besides these there are a vast number of legal treatises and commentaries based on ancient codes by modern lawyers, whose works are current and more or less esteemed as authorities in different parts of India."

The Five Schools of Hindu Law.—These are the schools of— 1. Bengal, 2. Benares, 3. Mithilá (North Behár and Tirhut), 4. Madras (Drávida), and 5. Bombay (*Mahā-ráshtra*). There are certain books regarded as special authorities in each of these principal schools.

" In Bengal the chief authoiities are the Mitákshará and Dáya-bhága (Treatise on Inheritance) developments of, or rather Commentaries on, Manu and Yájnavalkya. Although they profess to be based on these ancient books, they sometimes modify the laws there propounded to suit a more advanced social system."*

Institutes of Vishnu.—This has been translated by Professor Julius Jolly (*Sacred Books of the East*). It has very much in common with the Code of Manu. The translator says: " Of Slokas alone Vishnu has upwards of 160 in common with Manu, and in a far greater number of cases still his Sútras agree nearly word for word with the corresponding rules of Manu." (p. xxii). As already mentioned, it differs from Manu in being decidedly

---

* *Indian Wisdom,* pp. 300, 303.

sectarian. This feature is attributed to a Vishnavite editor, of a comparatively recent date (p. xxxii).

Sacred Laws of the Aryas.—Under this title are included vols. II. and XIV. of *The Sacred Books of the East.* They are described, "as taught in the schools of Apastamba, Gautama Vásishtha, and Baudháyana". The translator is the late Professor Bühler.

They differ in some minor points from Manu's Code; but the main contrast probably is the smaller space devoted to the duties of kings. In Manu, Bühler says :

" The description of the duties of the king, including the administration of justice and the civil and criminal law, occupies considerably more than one-third of the whole. For chapters vii-ix. contain no less than 982 verses, while the total number amounts to 2,682. None of the older law books devotes more than one-fourth of its text to such matters". (p. lv.) Burnell thinks that Manu was primarily intended as a manual for the Kshatriya. He says : " A question may perhaps arise here: If the text is intended as a manual for kings, why should so many details which refer solely to Brahmans be inserted ? The conclusive answer to this is that kings are bound to see that all do their *dharma* duty " (p. xxiv).

In the other treatises individual duties form the main subject

LAWS OF MANU.

LECTURE I.

Origin of the Book.—The great sages, having approached Manu, intent on one object, and duly saluted him, spoke as follows :—1.

'Deign, Lord, to tell us the rules of the four castes and of the intermediate ones. 2. For thou, Lord, alone knowest the whole ordinance of the Self-existent which is unattainable by reason and unlimited.' 3.

He whose power is measureless being thus requested by great sages, whose thoughts are profound, having duly saluted them, answered, 'Hear!' 4.

Creation of the Universe.—At first all was darkness, without definite qualities, undiscoverable, unknowable, as if immersed in deep sleep. 5. Then the Self-existent Lord, himself undiscernible, but making this universe discernible, appeared with undiminished glory, dispelling the gloom. 6.

He, wishing to produce various beings from his own body, first with a thought created the waters and cast his seed into them. 8. The *seed* became a golden egg, brilliant as the sun, and in it was born Brahmá, the great forefather of all the worlds. 9. Waters are called *náráh*, for they are the offspring of Nara ;* and since they were his first abode (*ayana*), he thence is called Náráyana. 10. From that eternal indiscernible cause was produced that male, famed in all worlds as Brahmá. 11. In that egg the divine One having dwelt for a whole year, at the close of which, by his thought alone, he split it into two. 12. Out of these halves he formed the heavens and the earth ; in the middle the sky, the eight points of the compass, and the eternal place of waters. 13.

From himself he drew forth mind (*manas*), which is and is not ; and from mind self-consciousness (*ahankára*), the ruler, the lord. 14. Likewise the great one, the soul, and all things with the three qualities and the five organs of sense, perceivers of sensible objects. 15. He having united minute particles of those six, of measureless power, with particles of himself, created all beings. 16.

---

* Another name for the Supreme Soul.

He, in the beginning, according to the words of the Veda, assigned to all creatures their names, actions, and conditions. 21.

From fire, wind, and the sun, Brahmá milked out the three-fold eternal Veda, called Rik, Yajus, and Sáman, for the due performance of sacrifice. 23.

He created times and the divisions of time, the lunar mansions, also the planets, rivers, oceans, mountains, plains, and uneven ground. 24.

To distinguish actions, he separated merit from demerit, and caused sentient beings to be affected by the pairs (of opposites), such as pleasure and pain. 26.

Whatever quality, noxious or innocent, gentle or savage, just or unjust, false or true he conferred on any being at its creation, the same quality clings to it (in future births). 29.

Creation of the Castes.—For the prosperity of the worlds he caused to proceed from his mouth, arms, thighs, and feet, the Brahman, Kshatriya, Vaisya, and Sudra, 31. Dividing his own body, he became half male and half female; and from that female he produced Viráj. 32. Know me, O most excellent of twice born men, to be that person whom Viráj, having performed austerities, produced by himself, to be the creator of all this world, 33. Then I, being desirous of creating beings, having practised severe austerities, first produced ten lords of created beings, great sages. 34. Marichi, Atri, Angiras, Pulastya, Pulaha, Kratu, Prachetas, Vasistha, Brigu and Nárada. 35. They, abundant in glory, produced seven other Manus, together with gods and classes of gods, and great sages, unlimited in power. 36. Yakshas, Rákshasas, Pisáchas, Gandharvas, Apsarasas, Asuras, Nágas, serpents, eagles, and the several classes of *pitris*, lightings and clouds, apes, fish, birds, reptiles, lice, fleas, biting gnats, and the several kinds of immovable things. 37-40.

Cattle, Rákshasas, Pisáchas and men are born from the womb; from eggs are born birds, reptiles, and fishes; from hot moisture spring stinging and biting insects *; plants are propagated by seed or slips. 43-46.

The different conditions in this ever-changing circle of births and deaths to which created beings are subject, begin with Brahmá, and end with those (just mentioned.) 50.

He whose power is incomprehensible having thus created the universe and me, was again absorbed into himself, alternating a time (of energy) by a time (of repose). 51. When that divine Being wakes, this world stirs; when he slumbers tranquilly, they all sleep. 52. When they are once absorbed in that great Being, he who is the soul of all beings placidly slumbers. 54.

---

* Insects are produced from eggs.

Then Brigu said that the seven glorious Manus, of whom Svayambhuva is the first, having produced all this universe, each ruled it in his own period. 63.

Measures of Time.—Eighteen winkings of the eye are one *kástha*; thirty *kásthás* one *kalá*; thirty *kalás* one *muhúrta*; and as many (*muhúrtas*) one day and night. 64.

A month is a day and a night of the *pitris*, but the division is by the lunar fortnights. The dark (half) (beginning with the full moon) is their day for action; and the bright (half, beginning with the new moon) is their night for sleep. 66.

A year is a day and a night of the gods. Their division. is this : their day is the northern and their night the southern course of the sun. 67.

Learn now the duration of a day and night of Brahmá, and of the several *yugas* in order. 68. Sages have given the name *Krita* to an age containing 4,000 years of the gods; the twilight preceding it consists of as many hundreds; and the twilight following it of the same number. 69. In the other three yugas, with their twilights preceding and following, are thousands and hundreds diminished by one. 70. Twelve thousand of such *yugas* are called a *yuga* of the gods. 71. A thousand of such divine *yugas* is a day of Brahmá, and a night is also the same in length. 72.

At the end of a day and night, he who was asleep, awakes, and awaking creates mind which is both real and unreal. 74. Mind, called into action by (Bramhá's) desire to create, performs again the work of creation; and thence first emerges ether, to which the learned ascribe the quality of sound. 75. From ether transforming itself springs air, the vehicle of all odours, that is held to have the quality of touch. 76. From air transforming itself arises light, making objects visible, dispelling darkness; with the quality of colour. 77. From light transforming itself (arises) water, with the quality of taste; and from water arises earth, with the quality of smell. 78.

The before-mentioned age of the gods of 12,000 years, if multiplied by 71, is called a *manvantara* (the period of a Manu). 79. Manvantaras, creations, and destructions, are numberless; the supreme Being does this again and again as if in sport.

. In the Krita age *dharma* stands on four feet and is complete, as is truth also; nor does any gain accrue to men from iniquity. 81. In the other (ages) by reason of (unjust) gains *dharma* is deprived successively of one foot; and through the prevalence of theft, falsehood, and fraud, merit is diminished by one-fourth (in each). 82.

Men, free from disease and prosperous, live 400 years in the Krita age; in the Tretá and other (ages) their life is lessened gradually by one quarter. 83.

In the *Krita* age the chief virtue is austerity; in the *Tretá*, knowledge ; in the *Dvápara,* sacrifice ; the only duty of the *Kali* is liberality. 86.

Duties of the Castes.—To preserve the universe the most glorious Being allotted separate duties to those who sprang from his mouth, arms, thighs, and feet. 87.   To Brahmans he ordained the duties of teaching, study, sacrifice and sacrificing (for others), also giving and receiving gifts. 88.   The duties of the Kshatriya were to protect the people, to bestow gifts, to study (the Vedas), and to abstain from sensual pleasures. 89.   The Vaisya, to tend cattle, give alms, sacrifice, study, trade, lend money, and cultivate land. 90. One duty only the Lord assigned to the Sudra, to serve meekly the other castes. 91.

Dignity of Brahmans.—Man is said to be purer above the navel ; hence the Self-existent declared the purest part of him to be his mouth. 92. Since the Brahmans sprang from the most excellent part ; since he was the first born, and since he possesses the Veda, he is by right the lord of this whole creation. 93.   Him, the Self-existent, after performing austerities, created from his own mouth, for presentation of offerings to the gods and *pitris,* and for the preservation of the universe. 94.   What being then can surpass him by whose mouth the gods and *pitris* eat offerings ? 95.

The birth of a Brahman is a constant incarnation of *dharma ;* for he exists for the sake of *dharma ;* and becomes one with Brahma. 98.   When a Brahman is born, he is the highest in the world, the lord of all creatures, to guard the treasury of *dharma.* 99.   Whatever exists in the universe is the property of the Brahman ; for on account of the eminence of his birth, the Brahman is entitled to it all. 100. The Brahman eats but his own food, wears but his own apparel, bestows but his own in alms ; other mortals exist through the benevolence of Brahmans. 101.

The Laws of Manu why Composed.—To settle his duties and those of the other castes. wise Manu, sprung from the Self-existent, composed this treatise. 102. It must be carefully studied by a learned Brahman and explained by him to his pupils, but not (be taught) by any other. 103.   This treatise produces everything auspicious ; it increases understanding ; it procures fame and lucky life, and leads to deliverance. 106.

Summary of Contents.—In this treatise *dharma* is fully declared ; also the good and bad qualities of human actions, and the perpetual usages of the four castes. The origin of the world, the ordinances of studentship, the laws of marriage and funeral rites, the modes of livelihood and the duties of a house-holder ; the laws concerning women, the whole *dharma* of kings, and the decision of lawsuits. The rules for examining witnesses, the laws concerning husband and wife, inheritance, gambling, and criminals, the rules regarding the service due by Vaisyas and Sudras, the origin of the mixed castes, and the rules of expiation, the threefold course of transmigrations, and final bliss, the eternal *dharma* of countries, castes, families, and rules concerning heretics. As Manu formerly in reply to my questions declared these Institutes, even so learn ye them to-day from me. Verses. 102-119.

LECTURE II.

Sources of the Law.—By *Sruti** (revelation) is meant the Veda ; by *Smriti*† (tradition) the law treatises (*dharma sástras*) : these two cannot be disputed. 10. The Veda, tradition, good custom, and one's own pleasure, they declare to be the fourfold means of defining *dharma*. 12.

Countries where the Law obtains.—The land between the divine rivers, Sarasvati and Drishadvatí, frequented by gods, the wise call Brahmávarta. 17. The plain of the Kurus, Matsya, Panchála, and Súrasena, form the region called Bramarshi, next Brahmávarta. 19. From a Brahman born in that country let all men learn their several usages. 20. That country which lies between the Himavat and Vindhya (mountains) which is to the east of Vinasana† and to the west of Prayága,‡ is called Madhya-desa, (the central region). 21. The land between those two mountains, (stretching) to the Eastern and Western oceans, the wise call Aryávarta. 22. Where the black antelope naturally grazes is fit for the performance of sacrifice ; beyond it is the land of the Mlechhas (barbarians). 23. Let twice-born men seek to dwell in those countries ; but a Sudra, distressed for a livelihood, may reside anywhere. 24.

The Sacraments.—Learn now the duties of the castes. 25. With auspicious rites prescribed by the Vedas must the ceremony on conception (*garbhádhána*) and other sacraments be performed for twice born men which purify them both here and hereafter. 26. By fire-offerings during pregnancy, by the birth ceremony, the shaving of the head to form a tuft, and by tying on the string of munja (grass) the taint derived from both parents is removed from twice born men. 27. By the study of the Vedas, by vows, by fire-offerings, by the *traividya* vow, by offerings, by offspring, by the great sacrifices and other rites, this body is rendered fit for union with Brahman. 28.

---

* *Sruti* means " what was heard ;" *Smriti*, " what was remembered."
† Where the Sarasvati disappears. ‡ Where the Yamuna and Ganges unite ; now Allahabad.

Before cutting the navel-string, the birth rite (must be per-formed, for a male child, and while mantras are being recited, he should be fed with honey and ghee from a gold (spoon). 29. The name-rite should be performed on the 10th or 12th day (after birth), or on a lucky day of the moon at a lucky hour, under an auspicious star. 30. Let the first part of a Brahman's name be auspicious, a Kshatriya's, denote power, a Vaishya's, wealth ; but a Sudra's, contempt. 31. The names of women should be agreeable, soft, clear, pleasing, auspicious, ending in long vowels, like words of benediction. 33.

In the fourth month the child should first be taken out of the house ; in the sixth month he should be fed with rice ; or any other custom thought auspicious by the tribe. 34. By command of the Veda, the *Kuda* rite (forming a tuft of hair) of all the twice born should be performed in the first or third year. 35. The investiture (with the sacred string) (*upanáyana*) of a Brahman should be per-formed in the 8th year after conception ; of a Kshatriya in the 11th ; of a Vaisya in the 12th. 37. Men who have not received investi-ture at the proper time become outcastes, and are despised by the respectable. 39. Let no Brahman, even in time of distress, form a connexion either through the Veda or by marriage with such impure men. 40.

The Dress of Students.—Let students, according to their castes, wear as upper garments the skins of black antelopes, deer or goats ; as under garments cloth made of hemp, flax or wool. 41. The girdle of a Brahman should be a triple cord of *munja*, smooth and soft ; that of a Kshatriya a bow-string made of *múrvi* ; that of a Vaisya, a triple thread of hemp. 42. The sacred thread of a Brahman should be of cotton threefold, put on (over the left shoulder) ; of a Kshatriya, of hemp thread ; of a Vaisya, of woollen thread. 44. A Brahman's staff should be of such a length as to reach his hair ; that of a Kshatriya to reach his forehead ; and that of a Vaisya to reach his nose. 46.

Asking Alms.—Having taken a staff to his liking, having worshipped the sun and walked round the fire from left to right, let the student beg alms according to rule. 48. Let him first beg food of his mother, or of his sister, or of his maternal aunt, or of some other female who will not disgrace him. 50.

Directions about Food.—Having collected as much food as he needs, and having informed his guru of it without guile, let him eat it after rinsing his mouth, with his face to the east. 51. If he seek long life he should eat with his face to the east ; if exalted fame, to the south ; if prosperity to the west ; if truth to the north. 52. Having eaten let him first rinse thrice his mouth with water, then twice wipe his mouth ; and lastly touch with water the hollow parts (of the head), the breast, and the head. 60.

Mode of Instruction.—The teacher having initiated a pupil, should instruct him in purifications, conduct, care of the sacred fire, and the *sandhyá* (twilight) devotions. 69. When about to recite the Vedas, let him rinse his mouth, as the law ordains; sitting with his face to the north; having made homage to the Vedas,.with a clean garment, and his senses subdued. 70. At the beginning and end of the recitation of the Veda, he must always clasp both the feet of his teacher; and he must study, joining his hands, for that is called homage to the Vedas. 71. When he begins to study let the teacher, always attentive, say, " Ho, recite l" and at the close of the lesson he must say, " Take rest." 73.

Recitation of Om, etc.—Let him always say *óm* at the beginning and end of. a lesson in the Veda; without *óm* before, it slips away; and without it after, it will not be retained. 74. Sitting on Kusa grass with their points to the east, purified by that holy grass, and by three suppressions of the breath, he may fitly pronounce *óm*. 75.

Prajápati milked out, *as it were*, from the three Vedas the letter A, the letter U, and the letter M, and the words *bhúh, bhuvah, svah*. 76. From the three Vedas also Prajápati, the Supreme Lord, milked out the three measures of that verse beginning with *tad*, called *gáyatrí*. 77. A Brahman, learned in the Vedas, who shall pronounce at both sandhyás, that syllable and that verse preceded by the three words, gains the merit of repeating the Vedas. 78.

The triliteral monosyllable (*óm*) is the supreme Brahma; suppressions of breath the highest austerity; but there is nothing more exalted than the gáyatri; truth is better than silence. 83. An offering of muttered prayer is ten times better than a regular sacrifice; a prayer, if unheard by any one, is a hundred times better; and a thousand times, if purely mental. 85.

Morning and Evening Prayer.—During the morning twilight let him stand muttering the sávitri till he sees the sun; in the evening let him mutter it seated till the stars appear. 101. He who stands repeating it in the morning removes all nocturnal sin; and seated in the evening repeating it destroys sin done in the day. 102.

Miscellaneous Duties.—Let a twice born man who has been invested, collect fuel, beg food, sleep on the ground, and do what pleases his teaches until he returns home, 108.

He who always salutes and reverences the aged obtains an increase of four things; life, knowledge, fame, strength. 121.

Way must be made for one in a carriage; for one above 90 years of age, a sick person, one carrying a burden, a woman, a student who has returned home, a king, and for a bridegroom. 138.

---

* Tat Savitur varenyam bhargo devasya dhímohi dhiyo yo nah prachodayát. It has been variously translated, but it is a prayer to the sun for his blessing.

Duties of a Student.—Day by day having bathed and being purified, let him pour out water to the gods, sages, and *pitris*, also let him worship the gods and collect fuel (for the sacred fire). 176. Let him abstain from honey, flesh, perfumes, garlands, juices, women, all sweets turned sour, and injuring living beings. 177. Ointments, collyrium for the eyes, sandals, carrying an umbrella, sensual desires, anger, covetousness, dancing, and music; 178. Gambling, disputes, backbiting, lying, looking at or embracing a woman, and hurting others. 179.

Let him fetch water, flowers, cowdung, earth, and Kusa grass as much as is needed by his teacher, and let him every day go out to beg. 182.

Commanded by his teacher, and even when not commanded, let him always study diligently, and do what is useful to his teacher. 191. Restraining his body, speech, organs of sense, his mind, let him stand with his hands joined, looking at the face of his teacher. 192.

By blaming his teacher, though justly, he will be born an ass; by falsely defaming him, a dog; by taking his goods, a worm; he who is envious (of his merit), an insect. 201.

Respect to Teachers and Parents.—A teacher is the image of Brahmá; a father, the image of Prajápati; a mother, the image of the earth; an (older) full brother, the image of one's self. 225. The pain and care which parents have in rearing children cannot be compensated in a hundred years. 227. Let every man always do what may please his parents and his teacher, for these three satisfied, he obtains all the rewards of austerities. 228.

By honouring his mother, he gains this world; by honouring his father, the middle (world); by obedience to his teacher, the Brahmá-world. 233. All duties are completely fulfilled by him who honours these three; but to him who respects them not, all rules are fruitless. 234.

End of Studentship.—Let not a student who knows the law present any gift to his teacher (before his return home); but when by his teacher's permission he is about to bathe for the last time, let him give to the venerable man according to his ability. 245. A field, gold, a cow, a horse, an umbrella, sandals, a stool, grain, clothes, (even) vegetables, and thus gain the remembrance of his teacher. 246. A Brahman who thus passes his studentship, without breaking his vows, ascends to the highest region, and will not be born again in this world. 249.

LECTURE III.

ON MARRIAGE AND ON THE RELIGIOUS DUTIES OF A HOUSEHOLDER,
OR THE SECOND STAGE OF LIFE.

Duty to Marry.—The study of the Vedas in the house of a teacher must be continued for 36 years, or for half that time, or for quarter of it, or only till mastery. 1. One who has not broken his vows as a student, after he has read the three Vedas or two, or even one only, should enter the order of householders. 2.

Choice of a Wife.—Let the twice-born man, having bathed, with the permission of his teacher and performed the stated ceremonies on his return home, marry a wife of the same caste, endowed with auspicious marks. 4. She who is not a Sapinda* on the mother's side, nor of the same *gotra* is his father, is eligible by a twice-born man for nuptial duties. 5. In connecting himself with a wife, the ten following families are to be avoided however great or rich in kine, goats, sheep, gold, and grain. 6. The family which neglects rites, which has no males, in which the Veda is not read, and the members of which have thick hair on the body, or have piles, or are afflicted with consumption, indigestion, epilepsy, white or black leprosy. 7. Let him not marry a maiden with reddish hair or having a redundant member ; one who is sickly, nor one without hair or with excessive hair, nor a chatterbox or one who has red eyes. 8. Nor one named after a star, a tree, or a river, nor one called after barbarians or a mountain, nor one named after a bird, a snake, or a slave, nor one with a name causing terror. 9. Let him choose for his wife a maiden free from bodily defects, who has a pleasant name, who walks gracefully like a *hamsa* or elephant ; whose hair is moderate, teeth small, and body soft. 10.

Caste Rules regarding Marriage.—For the first marriage of a twice-born man, a woman of the same caste is approved ; but for those who through lust marry again the following females are to be preferred. 12. A Sudra woman only must be the wife of a Sudra, she and a Vaisya, of a Vaisya ; these two and a Kshatriya of a Kshatriya ; these two and a Brahmani, of a Brahman.† 13. Twiceborn men, marrying, through folly, low caste women, soon degrade their families and children to the state of Sudras. 15. A Brahman who takes a Sudra woman to his bed, goes to the lower course ; if he beget a child by her, he loses his Brahmanhood. 17.

Eight Marriage Rites.—Now learn briefly the eight forms of marriage used by the four castes, some good and some bad in this world and in the next. 20. These are the rite of Brahma, the

---

* Related with six, in ascent or descent.

† These rules are now obsolete. Marriages are strictly limited between members of the same division of a caste.

gods, the Rishis, of Prajápati, of the Asuras, of the Gandharvas, of the Rákshasas, of the Pisáchas, the eighth and lowest. 21. Three of the five last are held to be lawful and two unlawful. The Pisácha and Asura (rites) must never be used. 25.

The gift of a daughter, voluntarily, with clothes and jewels, to one learned in the Vedas and of good character, is called the Brahma rite. 27. The gift of a daughter, after having adorned her, to a priest during the performance of a sacrifice, is called the Daiva rite. 28. When the father gives his daughter after having received a pair or two of cattle, according to law, that is termed the Arsha rite. 29. The Prajápatya rite is when the father gives his daughter with due honour, saying, 'May both of you perform together your duties!' 30. When the bridegroom gives voluntarily as much as he can to kinsmen and the maiden, that marriage is called Asura. 31. The voluntary connexion of a youth and a maiden which arises from lust is known as the Gandharva rite. 32. The seizure of a maiden by force from her home while she cries out and weeps after her kinsmen have been slain or wounded and their houses broken open, is called the Rákshasa rite. 33. When a man secretly embraces a damsel asleep, or intoxicated or disordered in intellect, that sinful marriage, called Pisácha, is the eighth and the basest. 34.

From the four marriages, Brahma and the like in order, are born sons learned in the Veda, and honoured by good men, rich, dutiful, who will live a hundred years. But of the remaining four marriages are born sons who are cruel and untruthful, abhorring the Vedas and duty. 39-41.

The Honour due to Women.—Women are to be honoured and adorned by their fathers, brothers, husbands, and brothers-in-law, who desire much prosperity. 55. Where women are honoured there the gods are pleased, but where they are not honoured all rites are fruitless. 56. When women are miserable, that family quickly perishes; but when they do not grieve, that family ever prospers. 57. Houses, cursed by women not honoured, perish utterly as if destroyed by magic. 58. Therefore let women be ever honoured at ceremonies and festivals with ornaments, apparel, and food, by men desirous of wealth. 59.

The Householder's Daily Rites.—With the marriage fire, the householder shall perform according to law the household rites, the five great sacrifices, and daily cook his food. 67. A householder has five slaughter-houses; the hearth, the grindstone, the broom, the pestle and mortar, the water-pot, by using which he is fettered (by sin) 68. For the expiation of all these, sages have ordained five great sacrifices to be daily performed by householders. 69. (These are as follows) Teaching and studying the Veda is the sacrifice to Brahma; offering cakes and water the sacrifice to the *pitris*; offering to fire, the sacrifice to the gods; offering of food, is the sacrifice to the Bhútas ; hospitality to guests is the sacrifice to men. 70. Whoever does not omit these five great sacrifices, if he is able, is untainted by the sins of the five slaughter-houses even though he constantly reside at home. 71. But whoever does not feed these five, the gods, guests, dependents, the *pitris*, and himself, lives not though he breathes. 72.

All dependent on the Householder.—As all creatures are supported by air, so all orders* of men are supported by the householder. 77. The sages, the *pitris*, the gods, the Bhútas, and guests also ask support from the householder : hence he who knows his duty must give each his due. 80.

Offerings to be made.—One should honour the sages by studying the Vedas ; the gods by offerings ; the *pitris* by shraddhas ; men by food, and the Bhútas by the Bali offering. 81. Daily should one perform a shraddha with food, or with water, or with milk, roots, and fruits; thus he pleases the *pitris*. 82. To all the gods assembled, let him throw up an offering into the air ; by day to the spirits going about by day ; and by night to the spirits going about by night. 90. On the house top let him make an offering for the welfare of all beings ; what remains let him give to the *pitris*, (casting it) to the south. 91. Let him drop gradually on the ground (the offering) for dogs, outcastes, those having grievous illnesses, crows, and insects. 92.

Almsgiving.—Having performed these offerings, he should cause his guest to eat before himself, and give a portion as the law ordains to a mendicant who studies the Vedas. 94. A twice-born householder by giving alms gains the same good fruit as a student who gives a cane to his teacher. 95.

Rules about Guests.—To a guest who has come one should give a seat and water and food according to his ability, after the due rites of courtesy. 99. A Brahman guest unhonoured takes away all the merit even of a man who lives on the gleanings of corn or even sacrifices in five fires. 100. Grass, earth (to sit on), water, and kindly speech as a fourth : these are never wanting in the houses of good men. 101.

Foolish householders who seek to live on the food of others become after death the cattle of the givers of such food. 104. A guest sent by the setting sun must not be turned away in the evening by a householder : whether he has come in time or out of (supper) time, let him not remain without food. 105. Let him not himself eat delicate food which he does not offer a guest : hospitality to a guest brings wealth, fame, long life, and heaven. 106. One should not hesitate to give food to brides, to infants, to the sick, and to pregnant women even before guests. 114. The idiot who first eats

---

* Students, householders, hermits, and mendicants.

himself without giving food to them does not know that after death he himself will be food for dogs and vultures. 115.

Some Rules about Shraddhas.—After performing the daily sacrifice to the pitris, a Brahman who keeps a sacred fire, should offer monthly at new moon the shraddha called *Pindánváháryaka.* 122. Sages call *anváhárya* the monthly shraddha to the pitris (to be offered after the cakes) and it is to be carefully performed with excellent meat. 123. I will now fully declare which Brahmans must be entertained at that ceremony and which must be avoided, and what food should be given. 124. As the shraddha of the gods he should feed two; at that to the pitris three, or one in both cases: even a rich man should not wish to have a large company,125.

Offerings to the gods and pitris should be presented only to a learned man alone; what is given to a most worthy Brahman bears great fruit. 128. As many mouthfuls as an unlearned man shall swallow at the offerings to the gods and pitris, so many red.hot iron balls must the giver swallow in the next world. 133. He whose shraddhas and offerings arise from friendship reaps after death no rewards for his shraddhas and offerings. 139. But a present duly offered to a learned man makes the giver and receiver partakers of the fruit, both in this world and the next. 143.

Who are not to be entertained at Shraddhas*.—Physicians, temple priests, sellers of flesh, and traders, must be shunned at offerings to the gods and pitris. 152. One who does not observe established customs, a eunuch, one who constantly begs, one who lives by agriculture, a club-footed man, and one despised by the virtuous, 165. A shepherd, a keeper of buffaloes, the husband of a twice-married woman; one who removes corpses—these are to be avoided with great care. 166. A blind man present destroys the reward of ninety; a one-eyed man of sixty; a leper of a hundred; one with a severe disease of a thousand. 177.

LECTURE IV.

A HOUSEHOLDER'S DUTY AS REGARDS SUBSISTENCE AND PRIVATE MORALS.

Means of Subsistence.—Let a Brahman having dwelt the first quarter of his life with a teacher, live the second quarter in his own house, after he has taken a wife. 1. Except in times of distress he should live by a calling which causes no injury ,or little injury to others. 2. To support life let him acquire property by the blameless occupations peculiar to his caste and without pain of body. 3. He may live by *rita* and *amríta* or by *mrita* and *pramrita,* or even by *satyánrita*; but never by *svavritti.* 4. By *rita* (truth)

---

* The list includes about sixty verses. Only a few are quoted.

is to be understood living by gleaning; *amrita* (undying) is (what is given) unasked; *mrita* (dead) is asked as alms; agriculture is *pramrita* (dead). 5. Trading is *satyánrita* (truth and lying); even by that also one may subsist; but service is termed *svavritti* (dog's-living) and should be avoided. 6.

Dress of Householder.—Having his hair, nails, and beard clipped, his passions subdued, with white clothes and pure, let him diligently study the Veda and engage in what will be for his welfare. 35. Let him carry a bamboo staff, a pot of water, a sacred thread, a handful of kusa grass, with a pair of bright gold rings in his ears. 36. He must not look on the sun, whether rising or setting, when eclipsed or reflected in water, or standing in the middle of the sky. 37. Let him not step over a rope to which a calf is tied; nor let him run when it rains, nor may he look at his own image in water: such is the rule. 38. Let him pass by with his right hand toward them a mound, a cow, an idol; a Brahman, ghee, honey, a cross-way, and well-known trees. 39.

Miscellaneous Rules.—Let him neither eat with his wife, nor look at her eating, or sneezing or yawning, or sitting at her ease. 43. Let him void his excrements by day with his face to the north; by night with his face to the south; at sunrise and sunset as by day, 50.

Let him not cast into water urine or ordure or saliva, or any thing soiled or blood or poison. 56.

Conduct towards a Sudra.—Let him not give advice to a Sudra, nor the remains of his meal, nor of ghee which has been offered. Nor may he teach him the law or explain to him expiation. 80. For he who teaches the law and enjoins expiations will sink together with that man into the hell called *Asamvritta* (unbounded), 81.

Gifts from an Avaricious King.—He who accepts a present from an avaricious King, a transgressor of the sacred law, will go in succession to the following 21 hells: 87.*

Reciting the Veda.—He must never recite the Veda indistinctly or in presence of Sudras; nor having recited the Veda in the last watch of the night, must be, though fatigued, sleep again. 99.

The new moon day destroys the teacher; the 14th, the pupils; the 8th and full moon destroy (recollection) of the Veda: hence one should avoid those days. 114.

The Rig-Veda is sacred to the gods; the Yajur-Veda to men; the Sáma-Veda is said to belong to the pitris, hence its sound is impure. 124.

---

* The names of the hells are given, some of them may be rendered as follows: Darkness, Burning, Gaping, Place of Iron Spikes, Thorny Tree, Sword-leaved Wood, Place of Iron Fetters, &c.

Should a cow, a frog, a cat, a dog, a snake, a mungoose or a rat pass between the teacher and his pupil; study is interrupted for a day and a night, 126.

Remembering former Births.—By constantly reading the Veda, by purity of body and mind and austerity, by doing no injury to living beings, one remembers his former births. 148. He who remembering his former births again recites the Veda, gains endless bliss by the constant study of the Vedas. 149.

Respect to the Aged.—Let him humbly greet old men (if they visit him) and give them his own seat. He should sit near them with joined hands, and when they leave walk some way behind them. 154.

Punishment of Assault.—Let him not, even when angry, lift a stick against another nor smite any one except a son or a pupil; these two he may beat to correct them. 164. A twiceborn man who merely threatens to hurt a Brahman shall be whirled about a century in the hell called *Támisra*. 165. Having intentionally struck him even with a blade of grass, he shall be born 21 times from sinful wombs. 166. He who foolishly draws blood from the body of a Brahman, who has not attacked him, will after death suffer severe pain. 167. As many particles of dust is the blood gathers up from the ground, so many years in the next world shall the shedder of blood be devoured by others. 168.

Wrong-doing punished in the End.—Iniquity committed in this life does not at once bear fruit, like the earth; but, advancing step by step, it tears up the root of the doer. 172. If (the punishment falls) not on himself, on his sons; if not on his sons, on his grandsons: wrong-doing never fails to bear fruit to the doer. 173. One grows rich, for a while, through iniquity, then he gains some advantage and overcomes foes; but at last he perishes from the root upwards. 174.

Gifts.—Though permitted to receive gifts, one should not be eager for them; by taking many presents, the divine light in him soon fades. 186. A wise man, without fully understanding the laws about gifts, should never accept a present, even though faint with hunger. 187. A man who knows not the laws, yet accepts gold or gems, land or house, cows, food, raiment, oils or ghee, becomes ashes like wood (in a fire). 188. Gold and food consume his life; land and a cow his body; a horse, his eyes; raiment, his skin; ghee, his strength; sesamum seed, his offspring. 189. A Brahman who is neither austere nor a reciter of the Veda, yet is eager to take a gift, sinks with it as with a stone-boat in the water. 190. As he who seeks to cross deep water in a stone-boat sinks to the bottom, so the ignorant giver and receiver sink down. 194.

Penalty of using what belongs to another.—He who uses without permission, a carriage, bed, seat, well, garden, takes upon himself one-fourth of the guilt of the sinner. 202.

Forbidden Food.*—Let him never eat food (given) by the insane, violent or sick; nor that on which lice have fallen, nor that intentionally touched by the foot. 207. Nor that of a blacksmith, of a Nisháda, an actor, a goldsmith, a basket-maker, or a dealer in weapons. 215. Food given by a king impairs vigour; a Sudra's food, spiritual excellence; a goldsmith's food, long life; that of a leather-worker, good name. 218. The food of an artizan destroys offspring; that of a washerman, strength; the food of a multitude or of harlots, excludes from heaven. 219.

Rewards of Gifts.—A giver of water gains freedom (from hunger and thirst); a giver of food, imperishable bliss; a giver of sesamum seeds, desired offspring; a giver of a lamp, best eyesight. 229. A giver of land obtains land; a giver of gold, long life; a giver of a house, most excellent mansions; a giver of silver, exquisite beauty. 230. A giver of clothes, a place in the world of the moon; a giver of a horse, a place in the world of the Asvins; a giver of an ox, eminent fortune; a giver of a cow, the world of the sun. 231. A giver of a carriage or bed, an excellent wife; a giver of protection, supreme dominion; a giver of grain, everlasting bliss; a giver of the Veda, union with Brahma. 232. Among all those gifts—water, food, cows, land, clothes, sesamum seeds, gold, ghee—that of the Veda is the most excellent. 233.

Dharma the only Secure Possession.—Giving no pain to any creature, let him collect merit by degrees, as white-ants raise their hillock, for the sake of a helper in the other world. 238. For in the next world neither father, nor mother, nor wife, nor sons, nor kinsmen, will be his companions: *dharma* alone remains. 239. Single is each being born; single he dies; single he receives the reward of his virtue; single also his bad deeds. 240. Leaving his dead body on the ground like a log of wood or a lump of clay, his kinsmen retire with averted faces; but his *dharma* follows him. 241.

Gifts which may be accepted.—Wood, water, roots, fruit, and food offered without asking, he may accept from all; also gifts of houses and protection. 247. Prajápati has declared that alms voluntarily brought unasked may be accepted even from a sinful man. 248. Of him who disdains to accept such gifts, neither will the *pitris* for fifteen years eat the offerings, nor will fire convey his oblations. 249. A bed, a house, horse, grass, perfumes, water, flowers, jewels, curds, grain, fish, milk, flesh, and vegetables, let him not reject. 250.

Close of Life as a Householder.—When he has duly paid his debts to the sages, to the *pitris*, and to the gods,† let him make over everything to his son, and reside in the house free from any

---

* There are 19 verses on this subject: only a few of which are quoted.

† To the sages, by Vedic study; to the *pitris*, by a son; to the gods, by sacrifice.

worldly concerns. 257. Alone let him ever meditate on the divine nature of the soul; for thus he will attain supreme bliss. 258· Thus has been declared the eternal rule of life of a Brahman householder, and also the rule for a student returned from his teacher, which cause an increase of goodness and are laudable. 259. A Brahman who lives always by these rules and is learned in the Vedas, daily destroys his sins, and will be exalted in Brahma's world. 260.

LECTURE V.

OF LAWFUL AND FORBIDDEN FOOD, IMPURITY, PURIFICATION, AND THE DUTIES OF WOMEN.

Why Brahmans die.—The sages having heard these laws for a returned student duly declared, thus addressed the great-souled Bhrigu, sprung from fire. 1: ' How, Lord, can death prevail over Brahmans who know the Veda and who fulfil their duties as they have been declared ?' 2. Righteous Bhrigu, the son of Manu, thus answered the great sages : Hear by what fault death desires to destroy Brahmans. 3. Death desires to destroy Brahmans through neglect of the Veda study, through breach of approved usages, through indolence, and eating forbidden food. 4.

LAWFUL AND FORBIDDEN FOOD.*

Garlic, onions, leeks and mushrooms and all vegetables arising from impurity are unfit to be eaten by the twice-born. 5. (Also) rice and pulse boiled together, wheat boiled in milk, rice-milk, cakes not prepared for a sacrifice, flesh not offered (to gods), the food of the gods and offerings. 7. Let every twice-born avoid carnivorous birds and such as live in towns, and quadrupeds with solid hoofs not allowed by the Veda, and the wagtail also. 11. The hedgehog, the porcupine, the iguana, the rhinoceros, the tortoise and the hare the wise have declared lawful food among five-toed animals; and all quadrupeds, camels excepted, which have but one row of teeth. 18. A twice-born man who intentionally eats mushrooms, a village pig, garlic, a tame cock, onions or leeks, becomes an outcast. 19.

Conflicting Rules regarding Flesh.†—Beasts and birds, prescribed, may be slain for sacrifice and for the support of dependents, since Agastya did this of old. 22. In the ancient sacrifices there were offerings of eatable beasts and birds and in the oblations of Brahmans and Kshatriyas. 23. One may eat flesh which has b͡ᴏᴏ͡

---

* The Rules occupy many verses ; only a few are quoted.

† Flesh was freely eaten in Vedic times, but Buddha forbidding the takin life, created in prejudice against it. In the time of Manu things were in a transi state.

consecrated, at the desire of Brahmans, when required by law, and in danger of life. 27. Prajápati created all that is, moveable or immoveable, for the support of life; all is food for the vital spirit. 28. No sin is committed by him who having honoured the gods and the pitris, eats flesh-meat which he has bought, or got himself, or which has been given him by another. 32.

As many hairs as grow on the beast, so many violent deaths shall the slayer of it, without a (lawful) reason, endure in the next world from birth to birth. 38. Svayambhu (the Self-existent) himself created animals for the sake of sacrifice ; sacrifice is for the good of the universe, therefore slaughter in sacrifice is no slaughter. 39. Plants, cattle, trees, amphibious animals, and birds which have been destroyed for the purpose of sacrifice, attain in the next world exalted births. 40. A twice-born man who, knowing the true meaning of the Veda, slays cattle for these purposes, causes himself and the cattle to reach the highest happiness. 42.

He who gives no creatures willingly the pain of confinement or death, but seeks the good of all, enjoys bliss without end. 46. Flesh cannot be obtained without injury to animals, and the slaughter of animals obstructs the way to heaven ; therefore one should avoid flesh. 48.

The permitter, the slaughterer, the butcher, the buyer, the seller, the cook, the server-up and the eater, are all slayers. 51. There is no greater sinner than the man who, without an oblation to the pitris or the gods, desires to increase his own flesh by the flesh of another creature. 52. He who during a hundred years annually performs the horse sacrifice and he who entirely abstains for flesh, enjoy for their virtue an equal reward. 53.

In eating flesh, in drinking intoxicating liquors, and in carnal intercourse there is no sin, for such enjoyments are natural ; but abstention from them produces great reward. 56.

PURIFICATION.

Purification of Living Beings.—When a child has teethed and when, after teething, his head has been shorn, and when he has been girt with the thread, and when being full grown he dies, all his kindred are impure ; on the birth of a child the law is the same. 58. Sapindas are rendered impure by a dead body for ten days, or until the gathering of the bones, or for three days or for one day only.* 59. Impurity on account of a death is ordained for all (sapindas) ; that caused by a birth (falls) on the parents alone ; (ten days') impurity for the mother ; the father becomes pure by bathing. 62.

---

* The number of days depends on what sort of a man the relative is.

3

A dead child, under two years of age, the relatives shall carry out, decked, and bury it in pure ground, without collecting the bones afterwards. 68. Such a child shall not be burnt with fire, and no libation of water shall be offered to it; leaving it like a piece of wood in the jungle, the kinsman shall be impure for three days only. 69.

Having heard after ten days of the death of a kinsman or the birth of a child, a man becomes pure by bathing in his garments. 77. He who has touched a chandála, a woman in her courses, an outcast, a women in child-bed, a corpse or one who has touched it, becomes pure by bathing. 85.

Let men carry out a dead Sudra by the southern town gate, but the twice-born by the western, northern, and eastern gates. 92.

A Brahman having performed funeral rites is purified by touching water; a Kshatriya by touching his horse or his arms; a Vaisya by touching his goad or the halter of his cattle; a Sudra by touching his stick. 99.

A Brahman have carried out, like a kinsman, a dead Brahman not a Sapinda or nearly related to his mother, becomes pure in three days. 101.

Knowledge (of Brahma), austerities, fire, holy food, earth, the mind, water, smearing with cow-dung, wind, prescribed rites, the sun, and time are purifiers of corporeal beings. 105.

The learned become purified by forgiveness of injuries; those who have committed forbidden acts, by liberality; those who have secret faults, by muttering (sacred texts; those who best know the Veda, by austerity. 107.

Rules for the Purification of Inanimate Objects.—Thus have you heard from me the rules for bodily purity: hear now the means of restoring purity to various (inanimate) things. 110.

The learned ordain that all articles made of brilliant metals, gems, and stone are to be purified with ashes, earth, and water. 111. Articles of copper, iron, bell-metal, brass, tin, and lead must be purified with alkalis, acids, or with water. 114. The purification of all liquids is by stirring them with kusa grass; of folded clothes by sprinkling; of wooden articles, planing, 115. Large quantities of grain and cloth are purified by sprinkling; small quantities are purified by washing them. 118. Leathern utensils and such as are made with cane must be purified like cloths; vegetables, roots, and fruits, like grain. 119. Grass, wood, and straw are purified by sprinkling water; a house by rubbing and smearing (with cow dung); earthen pots by a second burning. 122. But an earthen vessel which has been touched by spirituous liquor, wine, ordure, saliva, pus or blood, cannot be purified by another burning. 123. Land is purified by five ways, sweeping, smearing with cow-dung, sprinkling, scraping, and by cows staying on it. 124.

Manu declares the flesh of an animal killed by dogs is pure;

likewise the flesh of animals killed by carnivorous beasts; or by Chandálas and other Dasyus. 131.

Let each man sip water and sprinkle the cavities of the body after passing urine or ordure,when he is going to read the Veda, and always before taking food. 138. Although pure, let one sip water after sleeping, sneezing, eating, spitting, telling lies, and drinking water; likewise also when he is going to study the Veda. 145.

RULES ABOUT WOMEN.

Thus the rules of purification for men of all castes as well as the purification of things has been declared to you: hear now the laws for women. 146.

Women always under subjection.—Nothing must be done even in her own dwelling by a girl, or by a young woman, or by an aged woman, according to her own will. 147. In childhood, a female must be subject to her father; in youth, to her husband; on his death, to her sons: a woman must never be independent. 148 Never let her wish to separate herself from her father, her husband, or her sons; for by doing so she exposes both families to contempt. 149.

Duty to a Husband.—Him, to whom her father has given her, or her brother with the father's consent, let her honour while he lives, and when he dies let her never neglect him. 151. Though ill-behaved, though in love with another woman, or devoid of good qualities, yet a husband must constantly be revered as a god by a virtuous wife. 154. No sacrifice is allowed to women apart from their husbands, no religious rite, no fasting; as far only as a wife honours her lord, so far she is exalted in heaven. 155. A faithful wife who wishes to dwell (after death) with her husband must do nothing unkind to him, be he living or dead. 156.

Duties of Widows.—(When he is dead) she may emaciate her body by living on pure flowers, fruits and roots; but she must never even mention the name of another man. 157. Many thousands of Brahmans, chaste from their youth, though childless, have gone nevertheless to heaven. 159. Like these chaste men, a virtuous wife ascends to heaven, though childless, if after the death of her lord, she remain chaste. 160. But a widow, who from a wish to bear children is unfaithful to her dead husband, disgraces herself here, and loses her place with her husband (in heaven), 161. Off-spring begotten on a woman by any other than her husband is no offspring of hers; no more than a child begotten on the wife of another man (belongs to the begetter); nor is a second husband anywhere allowed to a virtuous woman. 162.

Miscellaneous Rules.—An unfaithful wife brings disgrace upon herself in this life; and (after death) she enters the womb of a jackal, and is tormented by diseases (the punishment) of sin, 164. She who slights not her lord, but restrains her thoughts, words and deeds, attains his abode (in heaven), and is called virtuous by the good. 165. A twice-born man must burn, with the sacred fire and sacrificial implements, a wife who dies before him of the same caste and of such behaviour. 167. Having thus kindled sacred fires and performed funeral rites to his wife who died before him, he may again marry, and kindle the fire. 168. Let him daily perform, according to the preceding rites, the five great sacrifices, and having taken a wife dwell in his house during the second period of his life. 169.

LECTURE VI.

ON THE THIRD AND FOURTH STAGES OF LIFE, OR THE HERMIT IN THE FOREST AND THE ASCETIC.

DUTIES OF THE HERMIT.

Having this remained in the order of a householder as the law ordains, let the twice-born, who had before completed his studentship, dwell in a forest, firm, and his organs wholly subdued. 1. When the father of a family sees wrinkles and gray hairs upon himself, and the sons of his sons, then let him seek refuge in a forest. 2. Abandoning all food eaten in towns, and all his utensils, let him repair to the forest, committing his wife to the care of his sons or with her also. 3. Taking with him the sacred fire and the implements for domestic sacrifice, he may depart from the village into the forest, and dwell there with his organs subdued. 4.

With various kinds of pure food, fit for ascetics, or with herbs, roots, and fruit let him offer the five great sacrifices according to rule. 5. Let him wear a skin or bark; let him bathe evening and morning; let his hair, beard, and nails never be clipped. 6. Let him give offerings with such food as he eats, and give alms according as he is able; and with presents of water, roots, and fruit, let him honour those who come to his hermitage. 7. Let him constantly recite the Veda, patient, well-disposed to all, composed, ever a giver and not a taker; compassionate to all living beings. 8.

With pure spring and autumn hermit rice collected by himself, let him prepare the sacrificial cakes and boiled grain according to rule. 11. Having presented to the gods that purest oblation from the forest, let him eat what remains, with salt made by himself.* 12. Let him not eat the produce of ploughed land although thrown

---

* Not sea salt, but salt made of salt earth.

away by any one, nor fruit nor roots grown in a village, even if oppressed by hunger. 16. Having procured food as he is able, he may eat it either at night or by day, or at every fourth or eighth meal-time. 19. Or, by the rules of the moon penance, eating a mouthful less during the bright fortnight, and a mouthful more each day during the dark fortnight; or he may eat only once at the close of each fortnight a mass of boiled gruel. 20. Or he may live always on flowers, fruits and roots, which have ripened by time, and have fallen of themselves, following the rule ordained for hermits. 21. He may roll on the ground or stand a whole day on tip-toe, or he may continue rising and sitting alternately; but at sunrise, noon, and sunset, he should bathe. 22. In the hot season let him sit exposed to five fires (four blazing around him, with the sun overhead) in the rains let him stand uncovered; in the cold season let him wear wet clothes, and let him by degrees increase his austerities. 23. When he bathes at sunrise, noon, and sunset, let him offer libations of water to the gods and pitris, and practising more severe ansterities, let him dry up his body. 24. Having, as the law directs, reposited those (three) fires in himself, let him live without a fire, houseless, silent, subsisting on roots and fruit. 25.

These and other rules must a Brahman living in the forest diligently practise; and to unite his soul with the Supreme Soul, let him study the various Upanishads. 29.

A Brahmin having got rid of his body by any of the modes which great sages practised,* is exalted in the Brahma world, free from sorrow and fear. 32.

DUTIES OF THE ASCETIC.

Having thus passed the third portion of his life in a forest, let him become a *sannyási* for the fourth portion of it, abandoning all worldly affections. 32. He who after passing from stage to stage (of life) having offered sacrifices and subdued his senses, becomes, tired of giving alms and offerings, a sannyási, attains bliss after death. 34. Having duly studied the Vedas, and legally begotten sons; having offered sacrifices according to his ability, he may fix his mind on liberation. 26. Having performed the prajápatya sacrifice with all his property as a gift, ;having reposited the sacred fires in himself, a Brahman may depart from his house. 38. Departing from his house, taking with him the means of purification, silent, unallured by the objects around him, let him wander about. 41. To attain felicity let him constantly dwell alone; seeing that the solitary man who neither forsakes nor is forsaken gains his end. 42. Without a fire, without a dwelling, he may go to a village for food; being indifferent to every thing, firm, meditating and fixing his attention on Brahma alone. 43. A potsherd (for an

---

* Drowning, falling over a precipice, burning or starving one's self.

alms' bowl), the roots of trees (for a dwelling), coarse clothing, entire solitude, and equanimity towards all creatures are the marks of one set free. 44.   Let him not wish for death ; let him not wish for life ; let him expect his appointed time as a hired servant expects his wages. 44.   Let him put down his foot purified by seeing (that there is no impurity in the way); let him drink water purified by a (straining) cloth ; let his speech by purified by truth ; let his heart be pure 46.   Let him never gain alms by (explaining) prodigies and omens, nor by astrology, nor giving advice, nor expounding holy texts. 60.

A gourd, a wooden bowl, an earthen dish, or a basket made of reeds, Manu, son of Svayambhu, declared to be vessels suitable, for a Sannyási. 54.   When there is no smoke, when the pestle lies motionless, when the fire has been extinguished, when people have eaten, and the dishes are removed, let the sannyási always beg food. 56.

Let him reflect on the transmigrations of men caused by their sinful deeds ; on their downfall into hell, and their torments in Yama's abode. 61.   And (let him reflect) on the departure of the soul from this body, and its new birth in another womb, and its wanderings through ten thousand millions of existences. 63.

To preserve living creatures, ever by day or night he should walk looking at the ground, even with pain to his body. 68. To expiate (the death) of those creatures which a sannyási may have unknowingly destroyed, let him bathe and make six suppressions of the breath. 69.   For as the dross of ores is consumed by fire, so the sinful acts of the organs are consumed by suppressions of the breath. 71.

A man possessing true insight is not fettered by his acts ; but he who possesses not that insight shall wander again through successive births. 74.   By not injuring any living creatures, by non-attachment of the organs, by the rules ordained in the Vedas, and by rigorous austerities men attain, even in this life, the state of beatitude. 75.

Let him quit this dwelling, with bones for its rafters and beams, with tendons for its cords ; with muscles and blood for mortar, with skin for its outward covering, which is foul-smelling, filled with urine and ordure ; infested by old age and sorrow, disturbed by sickness, harassed by pain, full of passion, and perishable. 76, 77.   He who leaves the body as a tree falls, or as a bird quits a tree, is delivered from the ravenous monster of the world. 78.   Leaving the merit of his good deeds to those who love him, and his evil deeds to those who hate him, he goes, through meditation, to the eternal Brahma. 79.   When he becomes truly indifferent to all objects, he gains everlasting happiness both in this world and after death. 80.

A Brahman who, with subdued mind, following the ten-fold

law, having discharged his three debts and heard the Upanishads, may become a sannyási. 94. Having given up all acts, and thrown off the guilt of his (sinful) acts, having subdued his senses and studied the Vedas, he may live at ease, in dependence on his son. 95. He who has thus relinquished acts—intent on his own duty, and free from desire, having effaced sin by renunciation, obtains the highest state. 96. Thus the fourfold law of Brahmans, which produces endless fruit after death, has been declared to you. Now learn the duty of Kings. 97.

LECTURE VII.

ON THE DUTIES OF KINGS AND THE SECOND CASTE.

The Greatness of Kings.—I will declare the duty of kings, and show how a king should conduct himself, how he was created, and how he can obtain his highest perfection. 1. A Kshatriya who has duly received Vedic investiture, must duly protect the whole (world). 2. Since, if this world had no king, it would tremble with fear, the Lord then created a king for the protection of all this (world). 3. Forming him of eternal particles drawn from Indra, Pavana, Yama, Súrya, of Agni and Varuna, of Chandra and Kuvera. 4. Since a King is composed of particles drawn from these chief deities, he surpasses all mortals in glory. 5. Even an infant king must not be despised from an idea that he is a mere mortal: no; he is a powerful deity who appears in human form. 8. Fire burns only one person who carelessly comes too near it; but the fire of a king in wrath burns a whole family, with its cattle and property. 9.

Punishments.—For the (king's) sake. I'svara formerly created his own son Punishment, the protector of all creatures, (an incarnation of) the law formed of the glory of Brahmá. 14. (Punishment) when rightly inflicted makes all people happy; but inflicted without consideration, it destroys every thing. 19. If the king did not untiringly punish the guilty, the stronger would roast the weak like fish on a spit. 20. The crow would eat the sacrificial cake, and the dog would lick the offering; ownership would remain with none; the lowest would usurp the place of the highest. 21.

A king who justly inflicts punishment prospers in those three (virtue, pleasure, wealth); but punishment itself shall destroy a king who is crafty, sensual, and base. 27. Punishment, very glorious, hard to be administered by men with unimproved minds, strikes down an unjust king, together with all his race. 28. Also

---

* Because they get no offerings.

it (destroys his) castles, his kingdom, the whole world, with immovable and movable things, and afflicts the Munis gone to heaven and the gods also. 29.

Aged Brahmans to be honoured.—Let the king, having risen at early dawn, reverence Brahmans learned in the Vedas and wise, and abide by their decision. 37. Constantly must he show respect to aged Brahmans, who know the Vedas and are pure; for he who always honours the aged is honoured even by Rákshasas. 38. From those versed in the Vedas, let him learn their triple doctrine; the primeval science of government, logic, and the knowledge of the (supreme) Soul; from the people he must learn practical acts. 43.

Vices to be shunned.—Let him carefully shun the ten vices proceeding from the love of pleasure, and eight springing from wrath, all ending in misery. 45. A king addicted to vices arising from a love of pleasure loses both his wealth and virtue; but given to those arising from anger, he may lose even his life. 46. Hunting, gambling, sleeping by day, censoriousness, excess with women, drunkenness, singing, music, dancing, and useless travel are the tenfold vices arising from love of pleasure. 47. Talebearing, violence, treachery, envy, detraction, slander, seizure of property, reviling, and assault, are the eight-fold vices to which anger gives birth. 48. Drinking, dice, women, and hunting let him consider to be, in order, the worst four in the set arising from love of pleasure. 50. Assault, defamation, and injury to property, let him consider the worst of the set arising from wrath. 51. Of death and vice, vice is the more dreadful; since after death a vicious man sinks from hell to hell, while a virtuous man reaches heaven. 53.

Appointment of Ministers.—Let him appoint seven or eight ministers, whose ancestors were royal servants, learned in the sciences; brave, skilled in the use of weapons, and of noble descent. 54. With them let him daily consider questions about peace and war, the *sthána*,* the revenue, protection, and bestowing aptly pious gifts. 56. Having ascertained the opinions of his counsellors, first apart and then all together, let him do what is most beneficial. 57. But with the most distinguished of them all, a learned Brahman, let the king confer on the most important affairs relating to the six measures. 58. To him, with full confidence, let him intrust all business; having taken his final resolutions with him, let him begin to act. 59. He should likewise appoint other officers, pure, wise, steady, gatherers of wealth by honourable means, well-tried. 60.

Appointment of an Ambassador.—Let him also appoint an ambassador, versed in the sciences, who understands hints, expressions of the face and gestures, honest, skilful, and of noble

---

* Army, Treasury, Capital, Kingdom.

birth. 63. For it is the ambassador alone who unites and divides; the ambassador transacts the business by which kingdoms are at variance or in amity. 66.

Advantages of a Hill Fort.—With all possible care let him secure a hill fort; for a hill fort possesses many superior advantages. 71. One archer on a wall is a match for a hundred below; a hundred for ten thousand; therefore a hill fort is recommended. 74. Let that fort be supplied with weapons, money, grain, beasts of burden, with Brahmans, artisans, engines, fodder, and water. 75. In the centre of it let him raise his own palace, well finished, protected, habitable in every season, resplendent, with water and trees. 76.

Marriage, etc.—Having prepared it, let him choose a consort of the same caste, with good marks, born of a great family, charming, possessing beauty and excellent qualities. 77. Let him appoint a domestic priest (*purohita*), and choose a sacrificial priest; these shall perform the family rites, and those for which three fires are required. 78.

Gifts to Brahmans.—Let him honour Brahmans returned from their teacher's house; for that (money given) is declared to be the imperishable Brahmanic treasure of kings. 82. It is a gem which neither thieves nor foes take away, which never perishes; kings must therefore deposit with Brahmans that indestructible jewel. 83. An offering made through the mouth of a Brahman is better than *agnihotras* (offerings to fire); it is never spilt, it never dries up; it is never consumed. 84. A gift to a non-Brahman (yields) equal fruit; to one who calls himself a Brahman, double; to a learned Brahman, a hundred thousand fold; to one who has read all the Vedas, endless recompense. 85.

War.—A king, who, while he protects his people is challenged by an enemy of equal, greater or less force, remembering his duty as a Kshatriya, must not shrink from battle. 87. Never to turn back in battle, to protect the people and honour Brahmans, are the highest duties of kings, and ensures their felicity. 88. Kings, who, seeking to slay each other, exert their utmost strength in battle and do not turn back, go to heaven. 89. Let no man in battle slay a foe with concealed weapons, nor with such as are barbed or poisoned, or are blazing with fire. 90. One (mounted) should not slay an enemy down in the ground, a eunuch, one with joined hands, one who (flees) with loosened hair, one seated, nor one who says "I am thine," 91. Nor one asleep, one unarmed, one naked, one without weapons, one not fighting, a spectator, one fighting with another. 91. Nor one whose weapons are broken, one in distress, one severely wounded, nor one afraid, one who fled: remembering virtue (one should not slay) them. 93. The soldier who flying in fear is killed by others, takes upon himself all the sins of his chief. 94. And whatever merit a soldier slain in flight may have gained, his chief takes all from him. 95.

Royal Policy.—Let him always act without guile, never treacherously; but keeping ever on his guard, let him discover the fraud intended by his foe. 104. Let not an enemy know his weak point, but let him know the weak point of his enemy; like a tortoise he should protect his members, and guard his own defect. 105. Like a heron, let him meditate on gaining advantage; like, a lion, let him put forth his strength; like a wolf, let him snatch (his prey); like a hare, he should retreat. 106. When he has thus prepared for conquest, let him subdue all opponents by negotiation and three other expedients.*
107. Among those four expedients the wise prefer negotiation and war for the prosperity of a kingdom. 107.

Appointment of Officials.—Let him appoint a lord of one town, a lord of ten towns, a lord of twenty, a lord of a hundred, and a lord of a thousand. 115. Let the lord of one town regularly report to the lord of ten towns the crimes committed in his time, and the lord of ten to the lord of twenty. 116. The lord of twenty shall report all to the lord of a hundred, and the lord of a hundred give information to the lord of a thousand. 117.

Such food, drink, and fuel as by law should be daily given to the king by the inhabitants of a town, let the lord of each town receive. 118. A lord of ten towns should enjoy two plough-lands; a lord over twenty, ten plough-lands; the lord of a hundred, that of a village; the lord of a thousand, a city. 119.

In every city let him appoint a superintendent of all affairs, high in rank, formidable, like a planet among the stars. 121. Let that (man) from time to time ever visit all those (other officials); and through his spies let him perfectly know their conduct in their several districts, 122. Since the servants of the king whom he has appointed guardians of district are generally knaves who seize what belongs to other men, from such he should protect his people. 123. Let the king confiscate the whole property and banish from his kingdom those evil-minded men who take money from suitors. 124. For women employed in the king's service and for his servants, let him daily provide maintenance suited to their station and to their work. 125. One *pana*† is to be given (daily) as wages to the lowest servant, six to the highest, with two cloths every six months, and a drona of grain every month. 126.

Taxes.—Having considered the rates of purchase and sale, the (length of) the way, the expenses for food and condiments, and the charges for the security of the goods, let the king make traders pay taxes. 127. A fiftieth part of cattle and gold may be taken

---

* Gifts, dissension, and force.
† A *pana* is the copper *fanam*, given daily. A *drona* was equal to 1024 handfuls.

by the king, an eighth part of grain, or the sixth or twelfth. 130. He may also take a sixth part of trees, meat, honey, ghee, perfumes, medicines, liquids, flowers, fruits, and roots. 131. Of leaves, herbs, grass, hides, cane work, earthen vessels and stoneware. 132. A king, though dying (from hunger), must not take taxes from a learned Brahman; nor must such a Brahman residing in his dominions perish from hunger, 133. The kingdom of that king where a learned Brahman suffers from hunger, will, ere long, be afflicted with famine. 134.

Let the king order a trifle to be paid, called a tax, by the common people of his realm, who live by petty trading. 137. Skilled workmen, artizans, and Sudras living by their labour, the king may cause to work for himself one (day) in each month. 138.

A King's Consultations.—Having risen in the last watch of the night, purified, and composed, having made oblations by fire and reverenced the Brahmans, let him enter the splendid audience hall. 145. Standing there, let him please his subjects before he dismisses them. Having dismissed all the people, let him take secret counsel with his chief minister. 146. Ascending the back of a hill or a terrace, or retiring to a lonely place or a forest, let him consult with them unobserved. 147. The despised, likewise (talking) birds, and especially women betray council: hence he must be careful among them. 150. At noon or midnight, when his fatigues are over and his cares dispersed, let him deliberate, either alone or with his ministers on virtue, pleasure, and wealth. 151. On the means of reconciling these things when opposed, on bestowing his daughters in marriage, and preserving his sons (from evil.) 152. On sending ambassadors and messengers, the probable results of his measures, on the behaviour of his women in the harem, and the doings of his spies. 153. On the whole eight-fold business of kings, and on the five classes (of spies) on the good will or enmity of his neighbours, and on the state of adjacent countries, let him reflect with the greatest attention. 154.

Royal Tactics.—Let him ever think of the six measures of a king, viz., alliance, war, marching, halting, dividing the army, and seeking protection. 160. He should endeavour to overcome his enemy by negotiations, by gifts, by creating divisions, either altogether or separately; never by battle. 198. Having conquered a country, let him worship its gods and honour righteous Brahmans; let him distribute gifts, and proclaim promises of safety, 201. All affairs are depending on the ordering of fate or on human acts; but of the two fate is unfathomable; in the case of men, action is known. 205. Let him preserve his wealth against misfortune; let him preserve his wife even at the expense of his wealth; let him at all events, save himself even at the cost of wife and wealth. 213.

Domestic Life.—Having consulted with his ministers in the manner before prescribed, taken exercise, and bathed, let the king enter his harem at noon to eat. 216. There let him eat food, well tested by faithful attendants, who know the proper time for dining, and not to be seduced, which has been (hallowed) by *mantras* which counteract poison. 217. Together with his food let him mix medicines which destroy poison, and let him always wear gems which repel it. 218. Let well-tried women, whose dress and ornaments have been examined, serve him with fans, water, and perfumes. 219. Thus let him be careful about his carriages, couches, seats, food, anointing, and all ornaments. 220. After dining he may divert himself with his wives in the harem; having idled, he must in due time again think of state affairs. 221. Dressed completely, he should again inspect his armed men, with all elephants, horses and cars, their accoutrements and weapons. 222. At sunset, having performed his devotions, let him, well armed, hear in an inner apartment what has been done by his reporters and spies. 223. Having dismissed these people, and gone to another private apartment, let him go attended by women, to the harem for food. 224. Having a second time eaten, cheered by music, let him take rest early, and rise refreshed. 225. A king, free from illness, should observe this system of rules; but if unwell, he may intrust all to his officers. 226.

LECTURE VIII.*

CIVIL AND CRIMINAL LAWS.

Duties of a King.—A king, desirous of inspecting suits, must enter his court of justice, composed and dignified, together with Brahmans and wise counsellers. 1. There, standing or seated, having stretched forth his right arm, without ostentation in his dress or ornaments, let him examine the affairs of suitors. 2. Daily he should decide, one after another, cases which fall under the eighteen titles, by arguments drawn from local usages, and written codes. 3. Of these (titles) the first is non-payment of debt (2) pledges; (3) sale without ownership; (4) partnership; (5) non-delivery. 4. (6) non-payment of wages; (7) breach of contracts; (8) revocation of sale and purchase; (9) disputes between master and servant. 5. (10) Disputes regarding boundaries; (11) Assault; (12) Slander; (13) Theft; (14) Violence; (15) Adultery. 6. (16) Duties of man and wife; (17) Partition; (18) Gambling and betting: these are the eighteen topics which give rise to lawsuits. 7. When the king cannot personally investigate suits, let him appoint a learned Brahman to try them. 9. Let that chief judge, with three assessors, having entered the court room consider all cases, sitting or standing. 10.

---

* This lecture is long; only the more interesting questions are noticed.

Need of Justice.—The only friend who follows men even after death is *dharma* : all else perishes with the body. 17.   One-fourth of (the guilt of) an unjust decision falls on the doer, one-fourth on his witnesses, one-fourth on all the judges, and one-fourth on the king. 18.   The realm of that king who looks on while a Sudra decides cases, will sink like a cow in a morass. 21.

Guides to a Decision.—By outward signs, let him see through the thoughts of men : and by their voice, colour, countenance, limbs, eyes, and action. 25.

Unknown Ownership.—Three years let the king detain property of which no owner appears ; the owner may claim it within three years ; but after that the king may take it. 30.

How Loans may be recovered.—By mediation of friends, by lawsuit, by artful management, by customary proceeding, and, fifthly, by force, a creditor may recover property lent. 49.

Witness-bearing.—One man free from covetousness may be the sole witness, and will have more weight than many women, because female understandings are apt to waver, or than many other men tarnished with crimes. 77.   A truthful witness gains (after death) exalted bliss, and the highest fame here below : such testimony is revered by Brahmá himself. 81.   The witness who speaks falsely shall be bound fast by Varuna's fetters during one hundred births : let men, therefore give no false testimony. 82.

The soul itself is its own witness ; the soul is the refuge of the soul.   Despise not therefore thy own soul, the supreme witness of men. 84.   The wicked say in their hearts, " None sees us ;" but the gods distinctly see them, and also the man within. 85.

In the forenoon, let the judge, being purified, call on the twice-born, being purified also, to declare the truth in the presence of the gods and Brahmans facing the north or the east. 87.   To a Brahman he must begin with saying. " Speak "; a Kshatriya, by saying, " Speak the truth ;" to a Vaishya *by comparing perjury to the crime of stealing* kine, grain or gold ; to a Sudra, by comparing it with every crime. 88.

If thou art not at variance with the divine Yama, son of Vivasvat, who dwells in thy breast, thou needest not go to the Ganges or Kurus* (to be purified). 92.   Naked and shorn, tormented with hunger and thirst, and deprived of sight shall the man, who gives false evidence, beg for food with a potsherd at the door of his enemy. 93.   Headlong, in utter darkness, shall that sinner fall into hell, who being questioned in court answers once falsely. 94.

When false witness is allowable.—In some cases a giver of false evidence from a pious motive, even though he know the truth, shall not lose a seat in heaven : such evidence wise men call

---

* The plains of the Kurus were considered sacred.

the speech of the gods. 103. Whenever the death of a Sudra, Vaisya, Kshatriya, or a Brahman would be caused by speaking the truth, |falsehood may be spoken: it is even preferable to truth. 104. In love affairs, at marriage, for the sake of grass for cows, or of fuel or to favour a Brahman, there is no sin in a (false) oath. 112.

Expiation of an allowable False Oath.—Those who wish fully to expiate the sin of such a falsehood should offer to Sarasvati an oblation of boiled rice. 105. Or let him pour ghee on the holy fire, according to rule, reciting the *Kúshmánda* texts, or that verse addressed to Varuna, 'Untie, O Varuna, the uppermost fetter,' or the three verses addressed to the waters. 106.

Verdict by an Oath.—In cases where no witness can be had, and the two parties contradict each other, the judge, unable to ascertain the truth, may discover it even by an oath. 109.

Trial by Ordeal.—Or (the judge) may cause him to hold fire, or dive under water, or let him touch the head of his wife and children. 144. He whom the blazing fire burns not, whom the water soon forces not up, or who meets with no speedy misfortune, must be held to be truthful in his testimony. 115. For formerly when Vatsa was accused by his younger brother,* the fire, the witness of the whole world, burned not even a hair, by reason of his veracity. 116.

Punishment of false Evidence.—He who perjures himself through covetousness shall be fined a thousand *panas*; if through distraction the lowest amount; if through fear, two medium fines; if through friendship, four times the lowest, 120. If through lust, ten times the lowest; if through wrath, three times the next; if through ignorance full two hundred; if through foolishness, a hundred only. 121. Let a just prince banish men of the three classes, if they give false evidence, having first levied the fine; but a Brahmin let him only banish. 123.

Kinds of Punishment.—Manu, son of the Self-existent, has named ten places of punishment in case of the three castes; but a Brahman must depart unhurt. 124. The privy parts, the belly, the tongue, the two hands, and fifthly the two feet; the eye, the nose, both ears, the property, and the body. 125.

Rates of Interest.—A money-lender, to increase his capital, may take the interest allowed by Vasishtha, one-eightieth part of a hundred a month. 140. Or he may take two per hundred remembering the duty of good men; for by taking two per cent. he becomes not a sinner for gain. 141. He may take a monthly interest of two per cent, three per cent, four per cent, five per cent. according to the order of the castes. 142. Interest beyond the legal rate cannot be recovered; the wise call it usury; the lender may not take more than five per cent. 152.

---

* Vatsa was accused by his younger brother of being the son of a Sudra woman.

Return of Purchases.—If any one in this world, after buying or selling anything, repent (of his bargain), he may give or take back such a thing within ten days. 222. But after ten days, he shall neither give it back nor take it back; if he take it back or give it back, he shall be fined six hundred (panas) by the King. 223.

Cattle Trespass.—Should cattle, attended by a herdsman, do damage in an enclosed field near a highway or the village, he shall be fined a hundred (panas), and the owner of the field should drive them off it without a keeper. 240. For damage done by a cow within ten days of her calving, by bulls or cattle of the gods, with or without a keeper, Manu has ordained no fine. 242.

Verbal Injuries.—A Kshatriya defaming a Brahma shall be fined a hundred (panas); a Vaisya a hundred and fifty or two hundred; but a Sudra shall suffer corporal punishment. 267. A Brahman shall be fined fifty if he slander a Kshatriya, twenty-five if a Vaisya, and twelve if a Sudra. 268. If a twice born man abuses a man of like caste the fine shall be twelve; but the fine shall be doubled for words that ought not to be uttered. 269. If a man of one birth insults a twice born man with gross invectives, he ought to have his tongue cut, for he sprang from the lowest part of Brahma. 270. If he mention, contemptuously, their names and castes, a red hot iron rod ten fingers long should be thrust into his mouth. 271. Should he, though pride, teach Brahmans their duty, the king shall order boiling oil to be dropped into his mouth and ear. 272. He who, even though he speak the truth, calls another man one-eyed, lame or the like, shall be fined at least in *kársápana*. 274. He who defames his mother, father, wife, brother, his son or his guru, shall be fined one hundred; and also he who does not give the right of way to his guru. 275.

Bodily Injuries.—With whatever member a low caste man injures a superior that member of his must be cut off; this is an ordinance of Manu. 279. He who raises his hand or a stick shall have his hand cut off; and he who in anger kicks with his foot, shall have his foot cut off. 280. A low caste men who tries to sit down by the side of a man of high caste shall be branded on the hip and banished, or the king may cause his buttock to be cut off. 281. If though pride, he spit on him, the king shall order both his lips to be cut off; should he urine on him, his penis; should he break wind against him, his anus. 282. If he seize (the Brahman) by the hair, let the king, without hesitation, cause both his hands to be cut off; also if he seize him by the feet, the beard, the neck, or the testicles. 283. If any man breaks the skin (of an equal) or fetches blood from him, he shall be fined one hundred; if he tears his flesh six *niskas*," he who breaks a bone shall be banished. 284. If a limb is injured or blood has been shed, the assailant shall pay the expense of a perfect cure, or shall pay the whole as a fine. 287.

Who may be beaten.—A wife, a son, a slave, a pupil, a younger brother, when they have committed faults, may be corrected with a cord or a cane, 299. But on the back part of the body (only) ; never on a noble part ; he who strikes them otherwise incurs the guilt of a thief. 300.

The King's share of Merit and Demerit.—A sixth part of the reward for virtuous deeds performed by the whole people belongs to the king who protects them ; but if he does not, a sixth part of their demerit also falls upon him. 304.

Punishment of Theft.—Corporal punishment shall be inflicted on him who steals more than ten measures of grain ; for less he shall pay eleven times as much, and shall pay to (the owner) the value of his property. 320. So shall corporal punishment be inflicted for stealing goods usually sold by weight, gold or silver and the like, or for stealing the finest garments. 321. For stealing more than fifty *palas*, cutting off the hand is enacted ; for less the king shall inflict a fine of eleven times the value. 322. For stealing men, and especially women, and very valuable gems, the thief deserves death. 323. For stealing cows belonging to Brahmans, for piercing the nostrils of a barren cow*, and for stealing (small) cattle, the offender shall instantly lose half of one foot. 325.

With whatever limb a thief commits an offence, among men, even that limb shall the king amputate for the prevention of similar crime. 334. In the case of theft the guilt of a Sudra is eight-fold ; that of a Vaisya sixteen fold ; and that of a Kshatriya thirty-two fold. 337. That of a Brahman sixty-four fold or even a full hundred ; or twice sixty-four fold, if he knows the nature of the offence. 338.

Right of Self-defence.—In self-defence, in a struggle for the fees of officiating priests, and in order to protect women and Brahmans, he who kills a man in a just cause does no wrong. 349. Let a man slay without hesitation any one attacking him with intent to murder, whether it be a guru, a child or aged man, or a very learned Brahman. 350. By killing an assassin, whether in public or private, no crime is committed by the slayer ; for thus anger meets anger. 351.

Punishment for Adultery.—Men who commit adultery with the wives of others, let the king banish, having punished them with such bodily marks as cause fear. 352.

Should a wife, proud of her family or (her own) excellence, violate the duty which she owes to her lord, the king shall cause her to be devoured by dogs in a public place. 371. Let him place the adulterer on an iron bed, well heated, under which logs shall be put till the offender is consumed. 372.

---

* Used for draught.

A Sudra committing adultery with a twice-born woman, guarded or not guarded, shall lose the part offending, and his whole substance if she was unguarded; everything, if guarded, 374. If a Vaisya or a Kshatriya commit adultery with an unguarded Brahmani, let the king fine the Vaisya five hundred panas, and the Kshatriya one thousand, 376. But these two committing adultery with a Brahmani who is guarded shall be punished like a Sudra, or be burned on a fire of dry grass, 377. A Brahman shall be fined one thousand if he forces a Brahmani who is guarded, but only five hundred if with her consent. 378.

Punishment of Brahmans.—Shaving the head is ordained for a Brahman instead of capital punishment; but in the case of the other castes, capital punishment may be inflicted. 378. Never shall the king slay a Brahman though convicted of all possible crimes; let him banish the offender from his realm, but with all his property and his body unhurt. 380. No greater crime is known in earth than slaying a Brahman; and the king therefore shall not even mentally consider his death. 381.

Fixing the Prices of Goods.—Let the king fix the rates for the sale and purchase of all marketable things; having duly considered whence they come, the length of time stored, what may be gained on them, and what has been expended. 401. Once in five days or once a fortnight, let the king settle the prices in the presence of these men. 402. Let all weights and measures be well tested; and every six months let them be re-examined.

A Sudra born for Servitude.—A Sudra, bought or unbought, a Brahman may compel to do servile work, for he was created by the Self-existent to be the slave of a Brahman. 413. Even if freed by his master, a Sudra is not relieved from servitude; since it is innate in him, who can set him free from it? 414. A Brahman may take the goods of a Sudra with perfect peace of mind, for as that slave can have no property, his master may take his goods. 417.

Who have no Property.—A wife, a son, a slave, these three are declared to have no property; whatever property they acquire is his to whom they belong. 416.

Duties of a King.—The king should carefully compel Vaisyas and Sudras to perform their respective duties; for by departing from them they throw the world into confusion. 418. Every day must the king look after public affairs, and enquire into the state of his horses, revenue, and expenditure, his mines, and his treasures. 419. A king who completes all these weighty affairs, and removes all sin, reaches the supreme path of bliss. 420.

LECTURE IX.

DUTIES OF HUSBAND AND WIFE, LAWS OF INHERITANCE, DUTIES OF A KING.

I will now declare the eternal duties of husband and wife, who keep to the path of duty, whether united or separated. 1.

Women to be kept in dependence.—Day and night should women be kept by the males of their families in a state of dependence. If they attach themselves to sensual enjoyment, they must be kept under the husband's control. 2. Their fathers must guard them in childhood, their husbands in youth, their sons in old age. A woman is never fit for independence. 3. Blamable is the father who gives not his daughter in marriage at the proper time; blamable is the husband who does not approach his wife 'in due season'; blamable is the son who does not protect his mother when her husband is dead. 4. Women must, above all, be restrained from evil inclinations, however trifling; for not being thus restrained, they bring sorrow on both families. 5. This is the highest duty of all castes: even weak husbands should strive to guard their wives. 6. He who diligently guards his wife, guards his posterity, his (ancestral) usages, his family, himself, and his *dharma*. 8.

Women how to be guarded.—No man can wholly guard women by force; but they may be restrained by the following expedients. 10. Let the husband keep his wife employed in collecting and spending money, in keeping things clean, in attending to her duty, in cooking food, and in looking after the household utensils. 11. Women are not guarded by being confined at home under trustworthy guardians; those women are truly secured who are guarded by their own good inclinations. 12.

Natural Disposition of Women.—Husbands, well knowing the disposition with which Prajápati formed women, should guard their wives with the greatest care. 16. Manu allotted to women a love of their bed, of their seat, of ornaments, impure desires, wrath, dishonesty, malice, and bad conduct, 17. For women no rite is performed with *mantras*,* thus the law is settled; women being weak and ignorant of vedic texts, are foul as falsehood itself: this is a fixed rule. 18. There are many texts sung even in the Vedas to make known the disposition of women : hear now their expiation for sin. 19, "If my mother going astray and unfaithful has sinned, may my father keep that seed from me." That is the scriptural text, 20. This expiation has been declared for every thought which enters her mind displeasing to her husband. 21.

---

* Except marriage.

A Wife possesses the Qualities of her Husband.—Whatever be the qualities of the man to whom a woman is united in marriage, such qualities even she assumes ; like a river united with the sea. 22. Thus Aksamálá, a woman of the lowest caste, when united to Vasishta, and Sárangi (when united) to Mandapála, became worthy of honour. 23.

Rules regarding Children.—Thus has the law, ever pure, between husband and wife been declared ; hear now the laws concerning children which are the cause of happiness in this world and the next. 25. When wives (*stríyah*) are blest because of offspring, worthy of honour, lamps in the house, there is no difference whatever between such homes and the goddesses of fortune (sríyah) 26. To bear children, the nurture of them when produced, and attention to the daily domestic affairs of life are peculiar to the wife. 27.

Offspring, the due performance of religious rites, attendance, the highest conjugal happiness, and heavenly bliss for ancestors and husband are dependent on the wife alone. 28. She who restrains her thoughts, speech and acts is not unfaithful to her lord, dwells with him (after death) in heaven, and in this world is called by the virtuous, a faithful (wife). 29. But a wife disloyal to her husband is disgraced in this life, and is born in the next of a jackal, and tormented by diseases which punish sin. 30.

No Release of a Wife from her Husband.—Neither by sale nor desertion can a wife be released from her husband : such we know to be the law which Prajápati made of old. 46. Once only is the partition of inheritance ; once is a damsel given in marriage, once does a man say, ' I will give' : each of these three is done once only. 47.

Niyoyga Allowed and Prohibited.—On failure of issue by the husband, a wife who has been authorized may obtain the desired offspring by a brother-in-law or some other *sapinda*. 59. The kinsman thus appointed, anointed with ghee, silent, shall beget at night one son, but never a second. 60. The purpose of the appointment having been fulfilled, these two shall behave towards each other like a father and daughter-in-law. 62.

By twice-born men no widow must be authorized to conceive by any other than her lord ; for those who authorise her violate the eternal law. 64. Such a commission is nowhere mentioned in the sacred texts on marriage ; nor is the marriage of a widow ever mentioned in the laws regarding marriage. 65. This practice, fit only for cattle, is reprehended by learned Brahmans ; yet it is declared to have been the practice even of men while Vena[X] ruled. 66. That chief of royal sages, possessing the whole earth, gave

---

* Vena is said to have been a wicked king, who demanded that sacrifices should be offered to himself instead of the gods.

rise to a confusion of castes, his intellect being destroyed by lust. 67. Since his time the virtuous blame that man, who, in delusion, appoints a woman whose husband is dead, to raise up offspring. 68.

When a Marriage Contract is Void.—Even after marrying a damsel according to rule, a man may abandon her if he find her blemished, diseased, or deflowered, or given to him by fraud. 72. If any man gives a maiden who has defects, without telling them, the bridegroom may annul that act of her evil-minded giver. 73.

The Time a wife should wait for a Husband.—If the husband went abroad for some sacred duty, she must wait for him eight years; if for learning or fame, six years ; if for pleasure three years. 76.*

When a second Wife may be taken.—A barren wife may be superseded in the eighth year ; she whose children are dead in the tenth ; she who bears only daughters in the eleventh ; she who is quarrelsome, without delay. 81. But a sickly wife who is loving and virtuous may be superseded (only) with her own consent, and must never be disgraced. 82. If a wife, legally superseded, shall leave her husband's home in anger, she shall instantly be confined or set aside in the presence of the family. 83.

Giving in Marriage.—A father should give his daughter in marriage according to rule, to an excellent and handsome youth of the same caste, even though she has not attained (the age of puberty). 88. But it is better that the damsel, though marriageable, should stay at home till her death than that he should give her in marriage to a bridegroom wanting in good qualities. 89.

When a Maid may choose her own Husband.—Three years let a damsel wait, though marriageable ; but after that term let her choose for herself a bridegroom of equal rank. 90. If not being given in marriage she choose her bridegroom, neither she nor the youth chosen commits any offence. 91. But a damsel who chooses for herself shall not carry with her the ornaments which she received from her father, her mother, or·brothers ; if she took them that would be theft. 92. He who takes to wife a marriageable girl shall not pay any marriage money to her father, since the father lost his right over her by hindering the natural result of her menses. 93.

Marriageable Ages.—A man thirty years of age may marry a girl of twelve who pleases him, or a man of twenty-four a damsel of eight ; if the performance of his duties would otherwise be hindered, let him marry sooner. 94.

Marriage Money not to be taken.—Even a Sudra should not take a marriage fee when he gives his daughter, for he who takes a fee virtually sells his daughter. 98.

---

* Some say that the wife should then go in search of her husband ; others, that she may marry again.

LAWS OF INHERITANCE.

Thus has been declared to you the law of husband and wife, founded on love, and the means of obtaining offspring : learn now the law of inheritance. 103.

Division of Inheritance.—After the death of the father and mother, the brothers, being assembled, may divide among themselves the paternal estate ; for they have no power over it while the parents live. 104. (Or) the eldest brother may take entire possession of the patrimony, the others living under him as under their father. 105. As soon as a son is born, a man becomes the father of a son, and is freed from his debt to the pitris ; that son therefore deserves the whole inheritance. 106. That son alone by whom he discharges his debt and through whom he attains immortality was begotten from a sense of duty : all the rest are considered as born of desire. 107. As a father supports his sons, so let the eldest support his younger brothers, and let them behave to the eldest as children to their father. 108.

Portions of Daughters.—Out of their respective shares the brothers shall give a fourth each to the (unmarried) daughters ; they who refuse shall be degraded. 118.

A Son through a Daughter.—He who has no son may appoint his daughter to raise up a son to him by the following rule : " The male child which may be hers shall perform my funeral rites." 127.

Personal Property of a Mother.—Property given to the mother on her marriage is inherited by her unmarried daughter alone ; and the son of an (appointed) daughter shall inherit the whole estate of (his maternal grandfather) without a son. 131.

But if after a daughter has been appointed a son be born (to her father), the division of the inheritance might in that case be equal ; since there is no right of primogeniture for a woman. 134.

Benefit of a Son.—Through a son one conquers worlds* ; through a son's son he obtains immortality, and though a son's grandson he attains the world of the sun. 137. Since a son delivers (trá-yate) the father from the hell called *put*, the son was therefore called *putra* by the Self-existent himself. 138.

Miscellaneous Rules.—The son of a Brahman, Kshatriya, or Vaisya by a Sudra wife receive no share of the inheritance : whatever his father give him, shall be his own. 155.

For a Sudra is ordained a wife of his own caste only ; all sons born of her shall have equal shares, though she have a hundred sons. 157.

---

* Heaven &c.

To three (ancestors) water must be offered; to three the funeral cake is ordained; the fourth (descendant) is the giver (of the water and cake); the fifth has no concern with them. 186.

The property of a Brahman must never be seized by the king; that is a settled rule. But the king may take the property of other castes on failure of all heirs. 189.

Property of Women.—What was given on the marriage fire, what was given in the bridal procession, what was given in token of love, what was received from her brother, mother or father, that is called the sixfold property of a woman. 194. A woman should never make a hoard from the goods of her kindred common to many; nor from her husband's property without permission. 199. Such ornaments as women wear during their husband's life time, the heirs shall not divide. They who divide them are degraded. 200.

Gains of Learning, &c.—Property (acquired) by learning belongs to him alone ,to whom it was given; likewise the gift of a friend, a present received at a marriage, or with the honey mixture. 206.

DUTIES OF A KING.

Gambling and Prize-fighting.*—Gambling and prize-fighting let the king exclude wholly from his realm; both cause the destruction of kingdoms. 221. Gambling and prize-fighting are the same as open theft; the king must ever be vigilant in repressing them. 222. Play by means of lifeless things is known among men as gambling; when living creatures are used, it is known as prize-fighting. 223. Let the king punish corporally all who indulge in gambling and prize-fighting or who abet them, also Súdras who assume the marks of the twice-born. 224. Gamblers, dancers, and singers, cruel men, heretics, men who do wrong acts, men who manufacture spirituous liquors, the king should banish at once from the city. 225.

Great Criminals.—The slayer of a Brahman, (a twice born) men who drinks sura, one who steals the gold of a Brahman, and he who defiles a Guru's bed, are to be regarded as great criminals. 235. On such of those four as have not performed an expiation, let the king ordain corporal punishment and fines according to law. 236. For defiling a Guru's bed, (the mark) of a female part shall be branded (on the forehead), for drinking sura, the sign of a tavern : for stealing the gold of a Brahman, a dog's foot; for murdering a Brahman, a headless corpse. 227. Such as have been branded with marks must be abandoned by their paternal and maternal relations, treated by none with pity or respect: such is the ordinance of Manu. 239.

---

* Betting. Bühler.

Uprooting thorn-like Men.—His realm having been put in order and forts built in accordance with the Institutes, (the king) should, with the utmost diligence, seek to uproot (bad men resembling) thorns. 252. Those who take bribes, cheats and rogues, gamblers, those who teach auspicious ceremonies, hypocrites, and fortune-tellers. 258.

Having detected these by means of trusty agents, who disguising themselves (pretend) to follow the same occupations, and by means of spies in different forms, let him bring them by artifice into his power. 261. By means of clever (men), formerly robbers (themselves) who well knowing the machinations of rogues, associate with them, let the king find them out and destroy them. 267.

Various Punishments.—Those who give no assistance when a town is being plundered, when a dike is breaking down, or a highway robbery committed, shall be banished with their effects. 274. The robbers who break through walls and commit theft at night, the king shall order their hands to be cut off and themselves impaled on a sharp stake. 276. Two fingers of a cut-purse the king shall cause to be cut off on his first conviction; on the second one hand and one foot; on the third he shall suffer death. 277. Those who give (to thieves) fire, food, arms or shelter, and receivers of stolen goods, let the king punish as he would thieves. 278. Those who break into a treasury, an arsenal, or a temple and those who steal elephants, horses or chariots, let him, without hesitation, destroy. 280. He who, except in case of necessity, drops filth in the king's highway, shall pay two *panas*, and remove the filth. 282. A fine of two hundred *panas* shall be imposed for all incantations intended to destroy life, for magic rites with roots performed by those not attaining their object, and for various kinds of sorcery. 290. But the king shall cause a dishonest goldsmith, the worst of all thorns, to be cut in pieces with sharp knives. 292.

Measures to be adopted.—By spies, by exerting his power, and by carrying out (various) enterprises, let a king constantly know both his own strength and that of his enemy. 298. Having first considered all the unfortunate accidents and injuries (possible) and their relative importance, let him begin his operations. 299. Though ever so much tried by repeated failures, and however weary he may be, let him renew his attempts again and again, for fortune favours the man who perseveres. 300.

The King identified with the ages.—All the ages, the Kríta, Tretá, Dvápara, and Kali, resemble the way in which a king behaves; for the king is called the age. 301. Asleep, he is Kali; awake the Dvápara (age); actively employed, the Tretá age; living virtuously, the Kríta age, 302.

Danger of wronging Brahmans.—Let him not, though in the greatest distress, provoke Brahmans to anger; for they, once enraged, could instantly destroy him, together with his army and equipments. 313. Who could escape destruction if he provoked them by whom the all-devouring fire was created, by whom the water of the sea was made undrinkable, and the waxing and waning moon. 314. Who could prosper if he injured those who, if angry, could create other worlds and regents of worlds, and deprive the gods of their divine station? 315. What man desirous of life would injure those by whom the worlds and the gods eternally exist and whose wealth is the Veda? 316. A Brahman, whether learned or ignorant, is a powerful divinity; even as fire is a great divinity whether applied (to the sacrifice) or not applied. 317.

A King should die in Battle.—Should a king be near his end, after giving all his wealth arising from fines to Brahmans, and committed his kingdom to his son, let him seek death in battle.* 323.

Duties of a Vaisya.—A Vaisya, after initiation, having married a wife should be constantly employed in gaining wealth and tending cattle. 326. For when Prajápati created cattle, he gave them over to the Vaisya, (while) he intrusted all people to the Brahmans and the king. 327. Let him exert himself most diligently to increase his property righteously, and let him zealously give food to all creatures. 333.

Duties of a Sudra.—The highest duty of a Sudra and that which leads to future bliss is to serve Brahmans learned in the Vedas and who (live) as householders. 334. If he be pure, obedient to the higher castes, mild in speech, never proud, ever seeking refuge in Brahmans, he attains (in his next life) a higher caste. 335. Thus has been declared, the excellent law for the conduct of the castes when they are not in distress for subsistence; learn their several duties in times of necessity. 336.

LECTURE X.

THE MIXED CASTES AND CLASSES : PROCEDURE IN TIME OF NEED.

The Three Castes.—Let the three twice-born castes, discharging their respective duties study (the Veda), but among them a Brahman alone should teach it, not the other two : this is an established rule. 1. The Brahman must know the means of subsistence ordained by law for all (the castes) ; he should declare them to the rest, and himself live according to (the law). 2. On account of his excellence, from superiority of origin, from his observance of restrctive rules and because of the difference of his initiation, the Brahman is lord of the castes. 3. The Brahman, Kshatriya, and

---

* If dying in battle is impossible, he should burn, drown, or starve himself.

Vaisya are the three twice-born castes, but the fourth, the Sudra, has one birth only. There is no fifth (caste). 4.

Origin of Low Castes.—From a Kshatriya and the daughter of a Sudra, springs a creature called an Ugra, resembling both Kshatriya and Sudra, ferocious in his manners, cruel in his acts. 9. From a Sudra are born by women of the Vaisya, Kshatriya and Brahman castes, by mixed castes, an Ayogava, a Ksattar, and a Chándála, the basest of men. 12. The mixture of castes is produced by adultery, by marriage with women who ought not to be married, and by the neglect of prescribed duties. 24. As a Sudra begets on a Brahman woman an outcast, so an outcast begets (a son) more outcast (than himself) by (women of) the four castes. 30. All those tribes of men which are excluded from those born from the mouth, the arms, the thigh and the foot (of Brahmá) ; are called Dasyus, whether they speak the language of the Mlechchas or that of the Aryas. 45.

Rules for Chandalas, etc.—The dwellings of Chándálas and Svapakas must be outside the village ; they should be deprived of dishes ; their sole wealth must be dogs and asses. 51. Their clothes should be the garments of the dead ; their dishes for food broken pots ; black iron their ornaments, and they must constantly wander about. 52. A man who regards his religious duty must not hold intercourse with them ; let their transactions be confined to themselves, and their marriages with their equals. 53. They shall always slay those who are to be slain by the sentence of the law and the king's order, and they shall take the clothes of the slain, their beds, and ornaments. 56. Desertion of life for the sake a Brahman or cow, without reward, or in defence of women or children, secures the beatitude of outcasts. 62.

Summary of Duties.—Avoiding all injury, veracity, not to steal, purity, and command over the bodily organs, Manu has declared this condensed rule for the four castes. 63.

Six Occupations of Brahmans.—Brahmans who are intent on union with Brahma, and firm in their duties shall live by six occupations, enumerated in their order. 74. Reading and teaching the Vedas, sacrificing and assisting others to sacrifice, giving and accepting gifts ; these are the six occupations for a Brahman. 75.

By selling flesh, lac, and salt a Brahman falls at once; by selling milk three days he sinks to the level of a Sudra. 92.

Agriculture to be avoided.—But a Brahman or a Kshatriya obliged to subsist by the occupations of a Vaisya should carefully avoid agriculture which causes great pain, and depends on others. 82. Some regard agriculture as excellent ; but by the virtuous this means of subsistence is blamed ; for the iron-mouthed wood injures the earth and the (creatures) dwelling in it. 93.

Forbidden Occupations.—A Kshatriya, in distress, may subsist by all these means ; but he must never have recourse to the highest functions. 95. A man of low caste who, through covetousness, lives by the acts of the highest, let the king strip of all his wealth and banish. 96. One's own duty, though defectively performed, is preferable to that of another completely performed; for he who lives by the duties of another caste, falls from his own. 97.

Any Food may be eaten in distress.—He who receives food when in danger of losing his life, from any man whatever, is no more tainted by sin than the sky by mud. 104. Ajagarta, suffering hunger, was going to slay his own son (Sunahsepha); yet was not tainted by sin since he only sought a remedy against famishing. 105. Vamadeva, who well knew right and wrong, was not rendered impure, when, oppressed with hunger, he desired to eat the flesh of a dog, for the preservation of his life. 106. Bharadwaja, eminent in devotion, when he and his son were almost starved in a lonely forest, accepted several cows from the carpenter Vradhu. 107. Moreover, Visvamitra, who well knew what is right and wrong, resolved, when oppressed by hunger, to eat the haunch of a dog, receiving it from the hands of a Chándála. 108.

Modes of Living.—There are seven virtuous means of acquiring wealth: inheritance, receiving, purchase, conquest, lending at interest, labour, and the acceptance of gifts from the good. 114. Learning, art, working for wages, service, rearing cattle, trade, agriculture, contentment (with little), alms, and receiving interest on money are ten means of subsistence (to all men in times of distress). 115.

A King's Dues.—A king who takes even a fourth part (of the crops) in time of distress commits no sin if he protects his people to the utmost of his power. 118. He may take from Vaisyas a tax of one-eighth on grain, and a tax of one-twentieth of their gains on money down to one *kársápana*. Sudras, artizans, and mechanics shall assist by their labour. 120.

Laws regarding Sudras.—Attendance on Brahmans is declared to be the best work of a Sudra: anything else will avail him nothing. 123. They must allot him a fit maintenance according to their own circumstances, after considering his ability, industry, and the number dependent on him for support. 124. The leavings of food should be given to him and old clothes; so too the refuse of grain and old household furniture. 125. A Sudra cannot commit sin, and he ought not to receive investiture; he has no right to fulfil the sacred law, but there is no restraint against his own duty. 126. No collection of wealth must be made by a Sudra, even though he be able; for a Sudra who has acquired wealth gives pain to Brahmans. 129.

The duties of the four castes in times of distress have thus been fully declared; by performing which exactly, they shall attain the highest beatitude. 130. Thus has been propounded the legal rules for the four castes; I will next declare the pure rule for expiations. 131.

LECTURE XI.

PENANCE, EXPIATION, ETC.

Who may drink Soma.—He who possesses food sufficient to support his dependents for three years or more, is worthy to drink soma. 7.

Who should not give gifts.—He who bestows gifts on strangers while he suffers his family to live in distress, although he has means, touches his lips with honey but swallows poison! such virtue is counterfeit. 9.

When goods may be taken.—Let him take that article required for the completion of sacrifice from the house of any Vaisya rich in cattle who neither sacrifices nor drinks Soma. 12. Or he may take, at pleasure, two or three articles required for sacrifice, from the house of a Sudra; for a Sudra has no business with sacrifices. 13. From the house of one who possesses a hundred cows but has no sacred fire, or one who has a thousand cows but performs no sacrifice, let a Brahman take, without hesitation, what is wanted. 14. The property of a Brahman should never be taken by a Kshatriya; but he who is starving may take the goods of any man who acts wickedly or who neglects his religious duties. 18. He who takes property from the bad and bestows it on the good, transforms himself into a boat, and carries over both. 19.

Punishment of a dishonest Brahman.—A Brahman who after begging goods for a sacrifice fails to offer the whole, shall become a crow or a kite for a hundred years. 25.

A Brahman's Weapons.—He may use, without hesitation, the powerful charms revealed by Atharvan and Angiras. The Brahman's weapon is speech; with that he may slay his enemies. 31.

Punishments in future Births.—A stealer of gold has diseased nails; a drinker of spirits, black teeth; the slayer of a Brahman consumption; the violator of his guru's bed, a skin disease. 49. A stealer of food, indigestion; a stealer of the words (of the Veda), dumbness; a thief of clothes, leprosy; a horse-stealer, lameness. 51. Thus according to the difference of their acts are born men despised by the good, stupid, dumb, blind, deaf, and deformed. 53.

Great Crimes.—Slaying a Brahman, drinking intoxicating liquors, stealing the gold of a Brahman, and committing adultery with the wife of a guru, and associating with such, are, they say, the great crimes. 55.

Secondary Crimes.—Stealing grain, base metals or cattle, intercourse with women who drink spirituous liquors, slaying a woman, a Sudra, a Vaisya, or a Kshatriya, non belief in a future state, are minor offences, 67.

Penance for slaying a Brahman.—For his purification the slayer of a Brahman should make a hut in a forest and dwell in it twelve

years, subsisting on alms, and making the skull of a dead man his flag.
73. Or, he may, of his own free will, become a mark to archers who
know (his intention), or he may cast himself thrice headlong into a
blazing fire. 74. For the preservation of a cow or a Brahman, let
him at once give up his life; since the preserver of a cow or a
Brahman atones for the crime of killing a Brahman. 80.

Punishment of a Brahman for drinking spirits.—A twice-born
man having foolishly drunk *surá*, shall drink that spirit boiling
hot: after his body has been severely burned, his offence is atoned
for. 91. Or he may drink boiling hot, until he die, cow's urine,
water, milk, ghee, or (liquid) cow-dung. 92.

Kinds of Spirituous Liquor.—Spirituous liquor should be
known to be of three kinds: that made of molasses, of (ground)
rice, and of the flowers of the Madhúca; as one, so are all forbidden
to the twice-born. 95.

Violating a Guru's bed.—He who has violated his Guru's bed,
shall, after confessing his guilt, extend himself on a heated iron-
bed—or embrace the red-hot image (of a woman); by death he
atones for his crime. 104.

Penance for killing a Cow.—He who has committed a minor
offence by killing a cow shall drink for a month barley gruel;
having been shorn, covering himself with the hide of the slain
one, let him live in a cow-house. 109. &c.

Penances for Murder.—For killing a Kshatriya, the penance
is one-fourth (part) of the penance for killing a Brahman, for
killing a Vaisya, one-eighth; for killing a virtuous Sudra one-
sixteenth. 127.

Penances for killing Sudras and animals.—The slayer of a
Sudra shall perform this whole penance* for six months; or he may
give to a Brahman ten white cows and a bull. 131. On killing a cat,
an ichneumon, a daw, a frog, a dog, a lizard, an owl, or a crow, he
must perform the penance required for killing a Sudra. 132. Or
let him drink milk for three nights, or walk a yojana, or bathe in
a river, or mutter the text addressed to the waters. 133.

If he kill a horse, he must give clothes; if an elephant five
black bulls; if a goat or a sheep, one bull; if an ass, a calf one year
old. 137.

Penances for Theft.—For a theft of eatables of various
kinds, a vehicle, a bed, a seat, of flowers, roots, and fruits, the
atonement is to (swallow) the five products of the cow. 166. For
stealing gems, pearls, coral, copper, silver, iron, brass or stone,
nothing but uncooked grains shall be swallowed for twelve days.
168. Drinking nothing but milk for three days is (the purification
for stealing) cotton, silk, wool, (animals) with cloven or single
hoofs, birds, perfumes, plants, or cordage. 169.

---

* Living in a jungle at the foot of a tree.

Various Penances.—By muttering with minds intent three thousand repetitions of the *Gayátrí* and by drinking milk for one month in a cow-house, one is freed from the sin of accepting presents from a bad man. 195.

On being bitten by a dog, jackal, ass, by village animals that eat flesh, or by men, horses, camels, and boars, one is purified by suppressing his breath (*Pránáyáma*). 200.

Punishment for Striking a Brahman.—An assaulter of a Brahman with intent to kill shall remain in hell a hundred years; for actually striking him a thousand. 207. As many particles of dust as the blood of a Brahman collects on the ground, for so many thousand years must the shedder of that blood be tormented in hell. 208.

Burning Penances.—The burning penance is (subsisting on) the urine of cows, cow-dung, milk, sour milk, ghee, kusa water for a whole day, and fasting for a night. 213.

Moon Penance.—If one diminishes his food by one mouthful each day during the dark fortnight, and increases it in the same proportion during the bright fortnight, bathing three times a day; this is called the moon penance. 217.

He who, with mind intent, for a whole month eats no more than thrice eighty mouthfuls of sacrificial food, dwells (after death) in the world of the moon. 221.

Benefit of Confession.—In proportion as a man voluntarily confesses wrong-doing, so far is he released from that offence like a snake from his slough. 229.

Benefits of Austerity.—All the bliss of gods and men is declared by the sages to whom the Veda was revealed, to have austerity for its root, austerity for its middle, and austerity for its end. 235. The sages who control themselves, subsisting on fruits, roots, and air; behold the three worlds with their movable and immovable (creatures) by their austerities alone. 237.

Whatever sin men commit in thought, word, or deed, they speedily consume by austerity, if they are rich in austerity. 242.

Benefit of Knowledge.—As fire instantly consumes with its bright flame fuel placed on it, so with the fire of knowledge he who knows the Vedas consumes all sin. 267.

Benefit of muttering Texts.—Even a drinker of spirituous liquors is absolved by muttering the hymn of Kutsa (beginning) with the word "away;" and the verse of Vasishtha (beginning) with the word "Toward," the Máhitra, and the (texts) containing the word "Purified." 250. He who has violated his guru's bed is cleared by repeatedly reciting the hymn beginning, "Drink the oblation," and that beginning with the words, "Not him," (and by) muttering the Purusha hymn. 252.

Value of remembering the Vedas.—A Brahman who retains in his memory the Rig-Veda is absolved from guilt, even if he had slain the inhabitants of the three worlds, and eaten food taken from anybody. 262.

LECTURE XII.

TRANSMIGRATION, SUPREME BLISS, AND DOUBTFUL POINTS OF LAW.

O sinless One, thou hast declared the whole system of duties ordained for the four castes ; explain to us now, truly, the ultimate retribution for their deeds. 1.

Sins of the Mind, Speech, and Body.—Coveting the property of others, thinking of forbidden things, and adherence to false (doctrines), are the three bad acts of the mind. 5. Abuse, falsehood, detraction, and useless tattle are the four bad acts of the tongue. 6. Taking things not given, injuring creatures without the sanction of law, and adultery with another man's wife, are the three bad acts of the body. 7.

For sinful acts committed with his body, a man becomes (in the next birth) something inanimate ; for sins of speech, a bird or a beast ; and in consequence of mental sins, of low birth. 9.

Rewards and Punishments.—If (the soul) practises virtue for the most part and vice to a small degree, it obtains bliss in heaven, clothed with a body formed of pure elementary particles. 20. But if it chiefly cleaves to vice and seldom to virtue, it suffers, deserted by the elements, the pains inflicted by Yama. 21. Having endured the torments inflicted by Yama, the Soul, its taint being removed, enters again those five elements, each in due proportion. 22.

Transmigrations.—Souls endowed with goodness attain always the state of deities ; those endowed with activity, the state of men ; and those endowed with darkness the nature of beasts : this is the triple order of transmigration. 40.

Immovable (beings), worms, insects, fishes, snakes, tortoises, cattle, jackals, are the lowest forms to which darkness leads. 42. Elephants, horses, Sudras, despicable Mlechchas, lions, tigers, and boars, are the middle states resulting from darkness. 43. Dancers and singers, birds, hypocrites, Rákshasas, and Pisáshas, are the highest of those produced by darkness. 43.

Kings and Kshatriyas, the domestic priests of kings, and men skilled in controversy, are the middle state caused by activity. 46.

Sacrificers, the sages, the gods, the Vedas, the constellations, the years, the pitris, and the Sádhyas are the middle orders caused, by goodness. 49.

Great criminals having passed through terrible hells during a great number of years, are condemned to the following births at the close of that period : 54. The slayer of a Brahman enters the womb of dogs, boars, asses, camels, cows, goats, sheep, stags, birds, Chándálas and Pukkasas. 55.

A Brahman who drinks *surá* enters the bodies of worms, insects, winged insects, (creatures) that eat ordure or of ravenous beasts. 56. A Brahman who steals the gold of a Brahman shall pass a thousand times into the bodies of spiders, snakes, chameleons, aquatic animals, and destructive Pisáshas. 57. He who violates the bed of his guru enters a hundred times the forms of grasses, shrubs and carnivorous animals, and those doing cruel acts. 58.

If a man steal grain, he shall be born a rat; if copper, a hamsa ; if water, a water bird; if honey, a stinging fly ; if milk, a crow ; if condiments, a dog ; if ghee, an ichneumon. 62. If a deer, or an elephant, he shall be born a wolf ; if a horse, a tiger ; if roots or fruits, an ape ; if a woman, a bear ; if water, a black-white cuckoo ; if carriages, a camel ; if cattle, a goat. 67.

With whatever disposition of mind a man performs any act, with that sort of body he reaps in each case the fruit. 81.

Acts which secure deliverance.—The results of acts have thus been explained : learn next those acts of a Brahman which lead to eternal bliss. 82. Study of the Veda, austerities, acquiring divine knowledge, control of the senses, doing no injury, and serving the Guru are the best means to obtain final happiness. 83. Is there among all these good acts performed in this world one more powerful than the rest in leading men to beatitude ? 84. Among all these holy acts the knowledge of the soul is said to be the highest ; because it ensures immortality. 85.

Two classes of Acts and their Consequences.—Acts connected with some desire (of benefit) here or hereafter, are called *pravritta,* such as prolong mundane existence ; acts without any desire for a reward, preceded by knowledge, are declared to be *nivritta* (such as cause the cessation) of mundane existence. 89.

He who performs acts leading to future births becomes equal to the gods ; but he who performs those causing the cessation of existence becomes exempt from a *body* composed of the five elements. 90.

Superiority of the Veda.—The Veda is the eternal eye of the pitris, gods, and men ; impassable and immeasurable is the Veda-ordinance : this is a sure proposition. 94. All those traditions (*smriti*) which are not grounded on the Veda, and the various despicable systems of philosophy produce no good fruit after death, for they are said to rest on darkness. 95.

Best means of securing Bliss.—Austerity and (Vedic) wisdom are the best means by which a Brahman can arrive at beatitude ; by austerities, he destroys guilt; by (Vedic) wisdom, one obtains the cessation of (births and deaths). 104.

Knowledge of the Atman or Self.—Let (every Brahman), concentrating his mind, fully recognise in the Self all things, both the real and the unreal, for he who recognises the universe in the Self, does not give his heart to unrighteousness. 118. The Self alone is the multitude of the gods, the universe rests on the Self ; for the Self produces the connexion of these embodied (spirits) with action. 119. He who thus recognises the Self through the Self in all created beings, becomes equal (minded) towards all, and enters the highest state, Brahman. 125.*

Benefit of reciting the Institutes of Manu.—A twice-born man who recites this Mánava treatise as it has been expounded by Brigu, will always be virtuous in conduct, and will reach whatever condition he desires. 126.

REVIEW OF THE LAWS OF MANU.

Sir William Jones, in the Preface to his translation, thus gives his general opinion of the treatise :—

" The work now presented to the *European* world, contains abundance of curious matter extremely interesting both to speculative lawyers and antiquaries, with many beauties, which need not be pointed out, and with blemishes, which cannot be justified or palliated. It is a system of despotism and priestcraft, both indeed limited by law, but artfully conspiring to give mutual support, though with mutual checks; it is filled with strange conceits in metaphysics and natural philosophy, with idle superstitions, and with a scheme of theology most obscurely figurative, and consequently liable to dangerous misconception ; it abounds with minute and childish formalities, with ceremonies generally absurd and often ridiculous ; the punishments are partial and fanciful, for some crimes dreadfully cruel, for others reprehensibly slight ; and the very morals, though rigid enough on the whole, are in one or two instances (as in the case of light oaths and of pious perjury) unaccountably relaxed.

" Nevertheless, a spirit of sublime devotion, of benevolence to mankind, and of amiable tenderness to all sentient creatures, pervades the whole work ; the style of it has a certain austere majesty, that sounds like the language of legislation and extorts a respectful awe ; the sentiments of independence on all beings but GOD, and the harsh admonitions even to kings, are truly noble."

EXCELLENCIES.

Where caste does not exert an influence, the laws are, in many cases, wise and just. Several great truths are acknowledged. A few examples may be given:

---

* From Bühler.

Wrong-doing punished in the End.—

Iniquity committed in this life does not at once bear fruit, like the earth; but, advancing step by step, it tears up the root of the doer. 172 If (the punishment falls) not on himself, on his sons; if not on his sons, on his grandsons: wrong-doing never fails to bear fruit to the doer. 173. One grows rich, for a while, through iniquity, then he gains some advantage and overcomes foes; but at last he perishes from the root upwards. 174. IV.

Dharma the only secure Possession.—

Single is each being born; single he dies; single he receives the reward of his virtue; single also his bad deeds. 240. Leaving his dead body on the ground like a log of wood or a lump of clay, his kinsmen retire with averted faces; but his *dharma* follows him. 241. IV.

The Voice of Conscience and God's Omniscience.—

The soul itself is its own witness; the soul is the refuge of the soul. Despise not therefore thy own soul, the supreme witness of men. 84. The wicked say in their hearts, "None sees us;" but the gods distinctly see them, and also the man within. 85. If thou thinkest: O friend of virtue, with respect to thyself, "I am alone," (know that) that sage who witnesses all virtuous acts and all crimes, ever resides in thy heart. 91. VIII.

Great moral duties are inculcated.

Respect to Parents and Teachers.—

The pain and care which parents have in rearing children cannot be compensated in a hundred years. 227. Let every man always do what may please his parents and his teacher, for these three satisfied, he obtains all the rewards of austerities. 228. By honouring his mother, he gains this world; by honouring his father, the middle (world); by obedience to his teacher, the Brahmá-world. 233. All duties are completely fulfilled by him who honours these three; but to him who respects them not, all rules are fruitless. 234. II.

Respect to the Aged.—

Let him humbly greet old men (if they visit him) and give them his own seat. He should sit near them with joined hands; and, when they leave, walk some way behind them. 154. IV.

Injuries not to be returned.—

Against an angry man let him not, in return, show anger; let him bless when he is cursed, and let him not utter speech, devoid of truth, scattered at the seven gates. 48. VI.

Duty of Hospitality.—

A guest sent by the setting sun must not be turned away in the evening by a householder: whether he has come in time or out of (supper) time, let him not remain without food. 105. Let him not himself eat delicate food which he does not offer a guest: hospitality to a guest brings wealth, fame, long life, and heaven. 106. III.

Caution against Religious Pride, etc.—

Let him not be proud of his austerities; let him not utter a falsehood after he has offered a sacrifice; let him not speak ill of Brahmans, though he be tormented (by them); when he has bestowed (a gift), let him not boast of it. 236. By falsehood a sacrifice becomes vain, by self-complacency (the reward for) austerities is lost, longevity by speaking evil of Brahmans, and (the reward of) a gift by boasting. 237. IV.

Vices to be shunned by a King.—

Let him carefully shun the ten vices proceeding from the love of pleasure, and eight springing from wrath, all ending in misery. 45. A king addicted to vices arising from a love of pleasure loses both his wealth and virtue; but given to those arising from anger, he may lose even his life. 46. Hunting, gambling, sleeping by day, censoriousness, excess with women, drunkenness, singing, music, dancing, and useless travel are the tenfold vices arising from love of pleasure. 47. Talebearing, violence, treachery, envy, detraction, slander, seizure of property, reviling, and assault, are the eight-fold vices to which anger gives birth. 48. Drinking, dice, women, and hunting let him consider to be, in order, the worst four in the set arising from love of pleasure. 50. Assault, defamation and injury to property, let him consider the worst of the set arising from wrath. 51. Of death and vice, vice is the more dreadful; since after death a vicious man sinks from hell to hell, while a virtuous man reaches heaven. 53. VII.

Guilt increased by Knowledge.—The idea is prevalent among Hindus that, " No blame attaches to the powerful;" the gods are above all law, and may do as they please. The Code opposes this immoral view :

In the case of theft the guilt of a Sudra is eight-fold; that of a Vaisya sixteen fold; and that of a Kshatriya thirty-two fold. 337. That of a Brahman sixty-four fold or even a full hundred; or twice sixty-four fold, if he knows the nature of the offence. 338. VIII.

Summary of Duties.—

Avoiding all injury, veracity, not to steal, purity, and command over the bodily organs, Manu has declared this condensed rule for the four castes. 63. X.

CONTRADICTORY TEACHING.

Flesh-eating.—In Vedic times cows were killed and beef was freely eaten. This is conclusively shown by Dr. Rajendra Lala Mitra in his *Indo-Aryans.* Buddha, about 2400 years ago, forbade the killing of animals, and as this found favour with the people, his teaching was adopted by the Brahmans. Manu's Code both allows and forbids the use of flesh. See Lecture v. 22—56, pp. 16, 17.

Niyoga allowed and forbidden.—Niyoga (rejoining) was the appointment of a kinsman to raise up issue by the wife of a childless husband or one deceased without leaving children. This custom existed among the Jews in ancient times and several other nations. In Section IX. 59-68, it is both sanctioned and prohibited. Dayanand Sarasvati advocated the practice.

There are many other contradictory statements.

DEFECTS.

While the excellencies of the Code attributed to Manu have been acknowledged, it must also be added that it contains much that is foolish, untrue, and unjust. The punishments, as stated by Sir William Jones, in some cases, "are reprehensibly slight," in others " dreadfully cruel."

Some illustrations will now be given.

VAIN SUPERSTITIONS.

About Food.—

If he seek long life, he should eat with his face to the east; if exalted fame to the south; if prosperity to the west; if truth to the north. II. 57.

What one eats with the head covered, what one eats facing the south, and what one eats with sandals on, that the evil demons eat. III. 238.

Calls of Nature.—

Let him void his excrements by day with his face to the north; by night with his face to the south; at sunrise and sunset as by day. IV. 50.

Directions might usefully be given about food and the disposal of filth; but the foregoing are simply foolish, and lead people to attend to ceremonies instead of what is of real importance.

Gems against Poisons.—It is the belief of ignorant Hindus that the wearing of certain gems is a safeguard against poison. This is supported in Manu's Code:

Together with his food let him mix medicines which destroy poison, and let him always wear gems which repel it. 218. VII.

FALSE BELIEF ABOUT A SON.

The Hindus are probably the only people in the world who believe that their future happiness in another world depends upon their having a son. The improvident marriages to which this belief gives rise are one great cause of Indian poverty. Sensible persons do not marry unless they see reasonable prospect of their being able to maintain a family.

A childless man who has no son to make offerings for him is said to fall into the hell, called *Put*. The Self-Existent is said to hold this to be true.

Since a son delivers (trá-yate) the father from the hell called *put*, the son was therefore called *putra* by the Self-existent himself. IX. 138.

This idea is a device of the Brahmans to get offerings at Shráddhas. Men are punished in another world on account of their own sins, not for the want of offerings.

INJUDICIOUS AND CRUEL PUNISHMENTS.

Punishment for Theft.—

" For stealing more than fifty *palas*, cutting off the hand is enacted." VIII. 322.

Theft is often the result of poverty. To cut off a thief's hand deprives him of the means of giving his livelihood in a honest manner. It was forbidden in Europe by the Justinian Code.

Punishment for Adultery.—

Should a wife, proud of her family or (her own) excellence, violate the duty which she owes to her lord, the king shall cause her to be devoured by dogs in a public place.   VIII. 371.

Punishment of Dishonest Goldsmiths.—

But the king shall cause a dishonest goldsmith, the worst of all thorns, to be cut in pieces with sharp knives.   IX. 292.

PALTERING WITH TRUTH.

Although truthfulness, in the abstract, is commended and lying condemned, the Code of Manu, like many other Hindu works, sanctions false oaths even on trifling occasions.

In love affairs, at marriage, for the sake of grass for cows, or of fuel or to favour a Brahman, there is no sin in a (false) oath.   VIII. 112.

Parallel passages from Vasishta and Gautama show that a *false* oath is here meant.   The wood is for sacrifice.

LOW REPRESENTATIONS OF WOMEN.

The position of women is a good test of the civilization of a country.   Amongst savages, women do all the hard work ; men, when they are not fighting or hunting, are smoking, drinking or sleeping.   The other extreme is in enlightened countries, where women are educated and treated with respect.   The position of women in India, like the position of India in the scale of civilization, lies midway between these two extremes.

Hindus, all over India, are said to be agreed on two points— the *sanctity of cows* and the *depravity of women*.   The Mahábhárata devotes hundreds of stanzas to prove the former.   Wilson says that " the greater number of Hindu tales turn upon the wickedness of women, the luxury, profligacy, treachery, the craft of the female sex."   Mr. D. E. Gimi says: " From the remotest times we have been systematically teaching the sex that they are most virtuous when they surrender all their rights, make no claims, and in every way submit themselves to the views and wishes, expressed and unexpressed, of their lord and master."   It is true that the Code of Manu enjoins mothers to be highly respected ; but low ideas are entertained of women as a sex.   The following are some illustrative extracts.

Women always to be under Control.—It is thought necessary always to guard them from temptation :

Day and night should women be kept by the males of their families in a state of dependence.   If they attach themselves to sensual enjoyment, they must be kept under the husband's control.   Their fathers must guard them in childhood, their husbands in youth, their sons in old age.   A woman is never fit for independence.   IX. 2, 3.

A wife may be beaten.—The words have been quoted, " Strike not even with a blossom, a wife guilty of a hundred faults." Manu says the opposite :

A wife, a son, a slave, a pupil, a younger brother, when they have committed faults, may be corrected with a cord or a cane. 299. But on the back part of the body (only); never on a noble part; he who strikes them otherwise incurs the guilt of a thief. 300. VIII.

Why women are to be honoured.

Women are to be honoured and adorned by their fathers, brothers, husbands, and brothers-in-law, who desire much prosperity. 55. Where women are honoured there the gods are pleased, but where they are not honoured, all rites are fruitless. 56. When women are miscrablo, that family quickly perishes; but when they do not grieve, that family ever prospers. 57. Houses, cursed by women not honoured, perish utterly as if destroyed by magic. 58. Therefore let women be ever honoured at ceremonies and festivals with ornaments, apparel, and food, by men desirous of wealth. III. 59.

When wives (*striyah*) are blest because of offspring, worthy of honour, lamps in the house, there is no difference whatever between such homes and the goddesses of fortune (*sriyah*) 26. IX.

Dr. Burnell remarks on the last quotation : " The lofty sentiment is however restricted by the clause ' because of offspring,' which is the sole reason from the standpoint of the law book why women deserve honour." The quotation from Book III. brings forward a still lower motive—the " desire of wealth."

Women ordained to be depraved.—

Manu allotted to women a love of their bed, of their seat, of their ornaments, impure desires, wrath, dishonesty, malice, and bad conduct. 17. IX.

The first three imply love of sleep, laziness, and vanity.

The Husband like the Wife's God.—

Though of bad conduct or debauched, or even devoid of (good) qualities, a husband must always be served like a god by a good wife. 154. V.

No Religious Duties for Women.—

No sacrifice is allowed to women apart from their husbands, no religious rite, no fasting; as far only as a wife honours her lord, so far she is exalted in heaven. 155. V.

For women no rite is performed with *mantras*, thus the law is settled; women being weak and ignorant of Vedic texts, are foul as falsehood itself : this is a fixed rule. 18. IX.

To gain the property of widows, the idea was given that they would become pre-eminently virtuous (*sati*) by being burned alive with the dead bodies of their husbands. The most blasphemous claim of the men is to be treated as the God of the women. It is true that they have not succeeded; but the guilt is all the same. The well-known lines of Tennyson express the truth :

" The woman's cause is man's ; they rise or sink
Together, dwarf'd or godlike, bond or free."

Men in India have sought to degrade women, but they have been drggged down to their level. The educated Hindu squanders money in ways which he knows to be idiotic; he joins in idolatrous ceremonies in which he thoroughly disbelieves, simply because he is under the sway of ignorant women. The grandmother is the true Kaiser-i-Hind or Empress of India.

Iniquitous Caste Rules.

At the outset, it may be remarked that Hinduism, properly speaking, is not a religion, but a social system, depending mainly upon food. Religion, in its primitive stage, may be defined as *the worship of higher powers;* more fully it is described as the performance of our duties of love and obedience towards God. But a Hindu may be an atheist, pantheist, polytheist, monotheist, he may be a materialist disbelieving entirely in " higher powers ;" yet if he conforms to the rules of caste, his status as a Hindu is unquestionable. It is the observance of caste rules which constitutes a man a Hindu.

The principal laws of the Code with reference to caste will now be noticed :

Origin of the Castes.—

For the prosperity of the worlds he caused to proceed from his mouth, arms, thighs, and feet, the Brahman, Kshatriya, Vaisya, and Sudra. 31. I.

Duties of the Castes.—

To preserve the universe the most glorious Being allotted separate duties to those who sprang from his mouth, arms, thighs, and feet 87. To Brahmans he ordained the duties of teaching, study, sacrifice and sacrificing (for others), also giving and receiving gifts. 88. The duties of the Kshatriya were to protect the people, to bestow gifts, to study (the Vedas), and to abstain from sensual pleasures. 89. The Vaisya, to tend cattle, give alms, sacrifice, study, trade, lend money, and cultivate land. 90. One duty only the Lord assigned to the Sudra, to serve meekly the other castes. 91. I.

Dignity of Brahmans.—

Man is said to be purer above the navel; hence the Self-existent declared the purest part of him to be his mouth. 92. Since the Brahmans sprang from the most excellent part; since he was the first born, and since he possesses the Veda, he is by right the lord of this whole creation. 93. Him, the Self-existent, after performing austerities, created from his own mouth, for presentation of offerings to the gods and *pitris,* and for the preservation of the universe. 94. What being then can surpass him by whose mouth the gods and *pitris* eat offerings? 95. I.

The birth of a Brahman is a constant incarnation of *dharma;* for he exists for the sake of *dharma ;* and becomes one with Brahma. 98. When a Brahman is born, he is the highest in the world, the lord of all creatures, to guard the treasury of *dharma.* 99. Whatever exists in the universe is the property of the Brahman; for on account of the eminence of his birth, the Brahman is entitled to it all. 100. The Brahman eats but his own food, wears but his own apparel, bestows but his own in alms ; other mortals exist through the benevolence of Brahmans. 101. I.

A Brahman, whether learned or ignorant, is a powerful divinity; even as fire is a great divinity, whether applied (to the sacrifice) or not applied. 317. IX.

Punishment of Brahmans.—

Shaving the head is ordained for a Brahman instead of capital punishment; but in the case of the other castes, capital punishment may be inflicted. 378. Never shall the king slay a Brahman though convicted of all possible crimes; let him banish the offender from his realm, but with all his property and his body unhurt. 380. No greater crime is known in earth than slaying a Brahman; and the king therefore shall not even mentally consider his death. 381. VIII.

A Sudra born for Servitude.—

A Sudra, bought or unbought, a Brahman may compel to do servile work, for he was created by the Self-existent to be the slave of a Brahman. 413. Even if freed by his master, a Sudra is not relieved from servitude; since it is innate in him, who can set him free from it? 414. A Brahman may take the goods of a Sudra with perfect peace of mind, for as that slave can have no property, his master may take his goods, 417. VIII.

Attendance on Brahmans is declared to be the best work of a Sudra : anything else will avail him nothing, 123. X.

No collection of wealth must be made by a Sudra, even though he be able; for a Sudra who has acquired wealth gives pain to Brahmans. 129. X.

Reward of Servitude.—

They must allot him a fit maintenance according to their own circumstances, after considering his ability, industry, and the number dependent on him for support. 124. The leavings of food should be given to him, and old clothes ; so too the refuse of grain and old household furniture. 125. X.

Punishment of Sudras.—

If a man of one birth insults a twice born man with gross invectives, he ought to have his tongue cut, for he sprang from the lowest part of Brahmá. 270. If he mention, contemptuously, their names and castes, a red hot iron rod, ten fingers long, should be thrust into his mouth. 271. Should he, though pride, teach Brahmans their duty, the king shall order boiling oil to be dropped into his mouth and ear. 272. VIII.

With whatever member a low caste man injures a superior, that member of his must be cut off : this is an ordinance of Manu. 279. He who raises his hand or a stick shall have his hand cut off ; and he who in anger kicks with his foot, shall have his foot cut off. 280. A low caste men who tries to sit down by the side of a man of high caste shall be branded on the hip and banished, or the king may cause his buttock to be cut off. 281. If through pride, he spit on him, the king shall order both his lips to be cut off ; should he urine on him, his penis ; should he break wind against him, his anus. 282. If he seize (the Brahman) by the hair, let the king, without hesitation, cause both his hands to be cut off ; also if he seize him by the feet, the beard, the neck, or the testicles. 283. VIII.

"National Congresses," regarded with enthusiasm, would be impossible under Manu's caste regulations. Sudras compose the great majority of the population ; but if they presumed to attend and sit in the presence of the "twice-born," banishment and mutilation would be the reward of their presumption.

Treatment of Certain Castes.—

The dwellings of Chándálas and Svapakas must be outside the village ; they should be deprived of dishes ; their sole wealth must be dogs and asses. 51. Their clothes should be the garments of the dead ; their dishes for food broken pots; black iron their ornaments, and they must constantly wander about. 52. X.

Sudras not to receive Religious Instruction.—

A Sudra cannot commit sin, and he ought not to receive investiture; he has no right to fulfil the sacred law, but there is no respect against his own duty. 126. X.

Let him not give advice to a Sudra, nor the remains of his meal, nor ghee which has been offered. Nor may he teach him the law or explain to' him expiation. 80. For he who teaches the law and enjoins expiations will sink together with that man into the hell called *Asamvritta* (unbounded). 81. IV.

Atonement for Killing a Sudra.—It is the same as for killing the following animals:

On killing a cat, an ichnuman, a daw, a frog, a dog, a lizard, an owl, or a crow, he must perform the penance required for killing a Sudra. 132. XI.

Support of Despotism.—The opinion of Sir William Jones has been mentioned that in the Code, " Despotism and priestcraft artfully conspire to give mutual support." In return for the privileges claimed by Brahmans, Kings are exalted to the level of Divinities:

I will declare the duty of kings, and show how a king should conduct himself, how he was created, and how he can obtain his highest perfection. 1. A Kshatriya who has duly received Vedic investiture, must duly protect the whole (world). 2. Since, if this world had no king, it would tremble with fear, the Lord then created a king for the protection of all this (world). 3. Forming him of eternal particles drawn from Indra, Pavana, Yama, Súrya, of Agni and Varuna, of Chandra and Kuvera. 4. Since a king is composed of particles drawn from these chief deities, he surpasses all mortals in glory. 5. Even an infant king must not be despised from an idea that he is a mere mortal: no; he is a powerful deity who appears in human form. 8. Fire burns only one person who carelessly comes too near it; but the fire of a king in wrath burns a whole family, with its cattle and property. 9. VII.

A king is an incarnation of the eight guardian deities of the world, the Moon, the Fire, the Sun, the Wind, Indra, the lords of wealth and water (Kuvera and Varuna), and Yama. 96. V.

Because the king is provided by (those) lords of the world, no impurity is ordained for him; for purity and impurity of mortals is caused and remained by (those) lords of the world. 97. V.

Discouragement of Foreign Commerce and useful Employment. Sudras, it is true, if necessary, may go anywhere, but the twice-born are restricted to Aryavarta:

That country which lies between the Himavat and Vindhya (mountains) which is to the east of Vinasana* and to the west of Prayága, is called Madhyadesa, (the central region). 21. The land between those two mountains, (stretching) to the Eastern and Western oceans, the wise call Aryávarta. 22. Where the black antelope naturally grazes is fit for the performance of sacrifice; beyond it is the land of the Mlechhas (barbarians). 23. Let twice-born men seek to dwell in those countries; but a Sudra, distressed for a livelihood, may reside anywhere. 24. II.

---

* The terminus of the Sarasvati.

" He who undertakes voyages by sea" (III. 158) is forbidden to be entertained at Shráddhas. Baudháyana is still stronger. Among the offences causing loss of caste (pataníya), the first named is " Making voyages by sea."*

England owes her wealth largely to her foreign commerce. The Parsis have prospered for the same reason. The prohitition of sea voyages has tended to the poverty of India.

Manu's Code discourages Agriculture :—

But a Brahman or a Kshatriya obliged to subsist by the occupations of a Vaisya should carefully avoid agriculture, which causes great pain, and depends on others. 82. Some regard agriculture as excellent; but by the virtuous this means of subsistence is blamed; for the iron-mouthed wood injures the earth and the (creatures) dwelling in it. 83. X.

Agriculture is the main wealth of a country. If it is wrong for the twice-born to engage in it, it must also be wrong for the Sudra. Thus, according to Manu, the people of India ought to starve. Even as it is, agriculture is discouraged by being left only to ignorant ryots.

According to Manu, carpenters (iv. 210), blacksmiths (iv. 215), oilmen (iii. 158), goldsmiths (iv. 215), architects (iii. 163), and physicians (iii. 152), are impure. The profession of a physician is most honourable and useful ; but the Code of Manu says, " The food of a physician (is as vile as) pus." iv. 220.

Dr. K. M. Banerjea says :—

" In civilized countries, every encouragement is held out to the cultivating of arts, especially the fine arts. Their professors are considered honourable—their labours are amply rewarded by men of taste and refinement. The pernicious system of caste taught a different lesson to the Hindus."

Dr. Banerjea quotes from the *Brahma Kaibuta Puràna* the reasons why certain castes were degraded :

Carpenter.—Born from Vishvakarma and a Sudra mother. Degraded by the curse of the Brahmans, whom he did not readily supply with wood necessary for a burnt offering.

Painter.—Vishvakarma and a Sudra mother. Degraded by the curse of the Brahmans for his faults in painting.

Goldsmith.—Degraded by the curse of the Brahman for stealing gold belonging to Brahmans.

Architect.—Born of a painter and a Sudra harlot. Degraded because base born.

Mlechcha.—Born of a Kshatriya father and Sudra mother. Begotten on a forbidden day.

Mlechchas are further described as " People born without the precincts of the ' excellent land of India,' whose ears are not bored, who are cruel, daring, invincible in battle, impure in practice, violent, and without religion."† " In their country the regenerate must not even temporarily dwell."

CONCLUDING REMARKS.

A review of the Code shows the correctness of its estimate by Sir William Jones. Though many of its laws are good ; yet, as a whole, it may be described as " a system of despotism and priest-craft, both indeed limited by law, but artfully conspiring to give mutual support, though with mutual checks."

The Code is marked by gross injustice between man and man wherever caste is concerned. Mr. R. C. Dutt says, " The caste system threw an indelible stain on the criminal law of India."*

The Laws of Manu are far inferior to the Penal Code of India. This, it is true, is what might be expected. The great charge against Manu's Code is its blasphemous claim to have proceeded from the " Self-Existent." Dr. K. M. Banerjea says : " Of all forgeries the most flagitious and profane is that which connects the name of the Almighty with an untruth." Principal Caird says that caste " involves the worst of all wrongs to humanity—that of hallowing evil by the authority and sanction of religion." " Instead of breaking down artificial barriers, waging war with false separations, softening divisions and undermining class hatreds and antipathies, religion becomes itself the very consecration of them."

The question who wrote the Code of Manu ? is easily answered by internal evidence. It was compiled by a tribe of Brahmans, called Mánavas, who lived in the country supposed to be rendered holy by the river Sarasvati. After framing a Code to gratify their pride and render all others subject to them, they pretended that it was given forth by their claimed divine progenitor Manu.

EVILS OF CASTE.

It is granted that caste has some advantages. It promotes a stationary semi-civilisation. It binds together men of the same class ; it promotes cleanliness, and it is a check, in certain directions, on moral conduct. But these are far more than counter-balanced by its pernicious effects. The opinions of competent witnesses will be given on this point.

Sir H. S. Maine, one of the ablest Europeans that ever came to India, in his *Ancient Law* describes Caste as " *the most disastrous and blighting of human institutions.*"

The following are the heads of a lecture by Pandit Sivanath Sastri on Caste :—

(1) It has produced disunion and discord.
(2) It has made honest manual labour contemptible in this country.
(3) It has checked internal and external commerce.

---

* *Ancient India.* Vol. II. p. 47.

(4) It has brought on physical degeneracy by confining marriage within narrow circles.

(5) It has been a source of conservatism in everything.

(6) It has suppressed the development of individuality and independence of character.

(7) It has helped in developing other injurious customs, such as early marriage, the charging of heavy matrimonial fees, &c.

(8) It has successfully restrained the growth and development of national worth; whilst allowing opportunity of mental and spiritual culture only to a limited number of privileged people, it has denied these opportunities to the majority of the lower classes, consequently it has made the country negatively a loser.

(9) It has made the country fit for foreign slavery by previously enslaving the people by the most abject spiritual tyranny.

Professor Bhandarkar says : "The caste system is at the root of the political slavery of India."

Keshub Chunder Sen says in an " Appeal to Young India :"—

" That Hindu caste is a frightful social scourge no one can deny. It has completely and hopelessly wrecked social unity, harmony, and happiness, and for centuries it has opposed all social progress. But few seem to think that it is not so much as a social but as a religious institution that it has become the great scourge it really is. As a system of absurd social distinctions, it is certainly pernicious. But when we view it on moral grounds it appears as a scandal to conscience, and an insult to humanity, and all our moral ideas and sentiments rise to execrate it, and to demand its immediate extermination. Caste is the bulwark of Hindu idolatry and the safeguard of Brahminical priesthood. It is an audacious and sacrilegious violation of God's law of human brotherhood. It makes civil distinctions inviolable divine institutions, and in the name of the Holy God sows perpetual discord and enmity among His children! It exalts one section of the people above the rest, gives the former, under the seal of divine sanction, the monopoly of education, religion and all the advantages of social pre-eminence, and visits them with the arbitrary authority of exercising a tyrannical sway over unfortunate and helpless millions of human souls, trampling them under their feet and holding them in a state of miserable servitude. It sets up the Brahminical order as the very vicegerents of the Deity and stamps the mass of the population as a degraded and unclean race, unworthy of manhood and unfit for heaven."

DUTY WITH REGARD TO CASTE.

1. **It should be made as widely known as possible that caste is not recognised in the Vedas.**

Professor Max Müller first printed the whole of the Rig-Veda with the commentary of Sayana; and he has devoted nearly his entire life to its study under the most favourable circumstances. What does he say?

"There is no authority whatever in the hymns of the Veda for the complicated system of castes. There is no law to prohibit the different classes of the people from living together, from eating and drinking together; no law to piohibit the marriage of people belonging to different castes; no law to brand the offspring of such marriages with an indelible stigma. Theie is no law to sanction the blasphemous pretensions of a priesthood to divine honours, or the degradation of any human being to a state below the animal." *Chips*, Vol. II.

2. **If caste is founded on a blasphemous falsehood and is unjust, it should be felt to be sinful to countenance it in any way.**

" Do men gather grapes of thorns or figs of thistles ? Neither can a corrupt tree bring forth good fruit." A system based on falsehood and characterised by gross injustice cannot have, on the whole, beneficial results.

3. **The Fatherhood of God and the Brotherhood of Man should be recognised and acted upon.**—An English poet says,

> " Children we are all
> Of one Great Father, in whatever clime
> His providence hath cast the seed of life;
> All tongues, all colours."

The Panchatantra has the following :—

> " Small souls inquire ,' Belongs this man
> To our own race, or class, or clan ? '
> But larger-hearted men embrace
> As brothers all the human race."

That there is no real distinction between men is admitted by all who have any claim to intelligence.

4. **No opprobrious Caste names should be used, and all should be addressed without indignity.**—The rudeness of some Europeans is a frequent cause of complaint; but no Englishman treats the Natives of this country with the contempt and insolence which high caste Hindus habitually display towards their low-caste brethren.

5. **Subdivisions of the same caste should freely eat together and intermarry.**—It is not desirable, as a rule, for persons widely dissimilar in social position and tastes to marry. In India when a man marries a wife, he is considered also to marry all her relations, who think they have a right to come and quarter themselves upon him. The first and easiest step is that proposed by Professor Runganatha Mudaliyar :—

" Can nothing be done to bring into intermarrying relations all the members of a class like Mudaliyars or Naidus? that the son of one Naidu should marry the daughter of another Naidu does not seem to involve any violation of the Veaic or Smritic precepts. No religious scruples need be set at rest, and I presume theie will be no great opposition from the priest. Custom is the only foe to contend with. I would fain think that if a small beginning were made in the way of uniting three or four of the many sections of Mudaliyars, the advantageous character of the union would be readily and fully appreciated, and the way be prepared for a further blending together of the sections that now stand apart."

6. Educated men of the same social standing should eat together and their families should intermarry.—This would be the second step in advance.

The great caste rod of terror is the prohibition of marriage. Hindus feel bound to marry their children, and if outcasted, this is impossible according to their ideas. There are now so many educated and intelligent Hindus in the great cities of India, that they outnumber several of the subdivisions that confine inter-marriage to themselves. A greater choice of marriage would thus be permitted, while there would also be a greater similarity of tastes and greater happiness. Early marriage would not be necessary, and girls might be properly educated.

It has been proposed that a union of this kind should be formed among educated men, who would bind themselves to inter-marry their children. If this were done, it would give a great impulse to the movement throughout India.

7. Educated men should refuse to make expiation.—One of the most degrading features of Hinduism is its *animal worship*. No doubt this has existed in all ages among savage or semi-civilized nations; but perhaps its lowest depth is reached in India. Not only is the cow worshipped, but her very excrements are consid-ered sacred. To swallow a pill composed of the five products of the cow will purify a man even from the deep pollution of a visit to England.

That the ignorant should cling to caste, is only what might be expected ; but it is humiliating that some men, who ought to be the leaders of enlightened public opinion, bend their necks to its yoke. Mr. Sherring says of such : " With all their weight of learning the possession of which enables them to carry off Univer-sity degrees and honours, they are perfectly content to mingle among the most superstitious and ignorant Hindus, to do as they do, to obey their foolish *dictum* as law, and to have no other aim in life than to conform to the most rigid usages of their ancestors."

The *Hindu Patriot,* the leading Native paper, while under the editorship of the late Hon. Kristo Das Pal, remarked :—

" As Indians, we should feel humilated to see any one of our fellow-Indians, with silly caste-notions in his head, travelling to Europe—especially, when the traveller pretends to represent the rising and educated classes of this great continent. We do not wish people in England, in Europe, to believe that what we call ' education ' has not yet freed our intellect from the trammels of superstition ; that we are afraid even to drink a glass of pure water from the hands of an Englishman, lest the recording angel should make a damning entry against us in his books ! India can never be regenerated till she has outlived the oppressive institution of caste ; and she can never outlive the oppressive system of caste, if we are to look to men like . . . . who begins like a daring rebel, but ends an imbecile swallower of penitential pills ! "

All Indians, however, on their return from England, have not acted the part of the poltroon. One good result has been that it is beginning to be admitted that expiation is not necessary.

Appeal of the Indra Prakash.—Some years ago the following just remarks appeared in this influential Bombay Journal:—

" The question is not about going to England, but about an unmanly submission to the vilest and most absurd prejudices of the caste system and Hinduism, which nothing can check and uproot but a spirit of noble independence, rigid moral firmness, and genuine patriotism. The prohibition to go to England is the least of our complaints against the tyranny of caste."

" It extends from the most trifling to the most important affairs of Hindu life. It cripples the independent action of individuals, sows the seed of bitter discord between the different sections of society, encourages the most abominable practices, and dries up all the springs of that social, moral, and intellectual freedom which alone can secure greatness, whether to individuals or nations."

" Oh God, have mercy on our fallen-countrymen ! Give them true knowledge of Thy Fatherhood, and their brotherhood ; that our countless millions may be bound by one social tie, and joining hand with hand, and heart with heart, move onward in the path of freedom and righteousness, knowledge and glory, and national regeneration."

A SHORT AND PERFECT CODE.

The Lord Jesus Christ summed up the whole law in two commandments :

" Thou shalt love the Lord thy God with all thy heart, and with all thy soul, and with all thy mind. This is the first and great commandment.

" And the second is like unto it, Thou shalt love thy neighbour as thyself. *Matthew*, xxii. 37—39."

The whole indeed is included in one word, LOVE.

Read the New Testament and it will be seen how Jesus Christ explained these two great laws by His example ; how pardon for the past breach of them may be obtained, and strength to observe them better in time to come.

Individual Responsibility.

The solemn words of Manu's Code may again be quoted :

Single is each being born ; single he dies ; single he receives the reward of his virtue ; single also his bad deeds. 240. Leaving his dead body on the ground like a log of wood or a lump of clay, his kinsmen retire with averted faces ; but his *dharma* follows him. 241. IV.

We should therefore do what is right, irrespective of the conduct of relatives or any others.

www.ingramcontent.com/pod-product-compliance
Lightning Source LLC
Chambersburg PA
CBHW070547160726
48003CB00005B/1938